Retired?

You must be joking

Beatrice Holloway

TSL Publications

First published in Great Britain in 2021
By TSL Publications, Rickmansworth

Copyright © 2021 Beatrice Holloway
Cover: adapted from:
https://pixabay.com/illustrations/grandma-granny-gran-rocking-chair-486796/ and https://pixabay.com/illustrations/mind-mapping-icon-thinking-mind-map-5597528/

ISBN / 978-1-913294-88-5

Acknowledgements

Dave Ferris for cartoon Page 166

Gill Richiardi for a good and helpful friend.

And, as always, TSL publications Directors, Anne and John, for their continuous interest in my work support and unstinting advice.

About Beatrice

This is the fourth of Beatrice's adult books. Her other book titles are: *A Man from the North East, Elusive Destiny* and *Archie's Children*. Beatrice has also written a number of children's books including three telling of the adventures of a boy's life on the canals during the early twentieth century. Following these are six books about a boy's childhood in Wales during the difficult times of the 1970s. All are available as ebooks.

The London Borough of Hillingdon library service has published two of her children's stories and the Hillingdon Arts Association awarded her a Certificate of merit – 'In recognition of an outstanding contribution to the Arts'.

Beatrice was awarded a Lottery Grant to write a commissioned historical play: *From Commoner to Coronet*.

Beatrice now has another five short plays published.

She is a retired teacher and a member of The Society of Women Writers and Journalists and the Society of Authors. She has been a member of a local writing group – Phrase Writers – for over twenty years and is the children's storyteller for Hillingdon Narrowboats Association.

Retired?
You must be joking

Confused by the title? Speak to retirees and most will tell you, 'Never been so busy in all of my life!'

This little book is really an anthology of my work since I retired some twenty years ago. It is said that reading and listening to stories can take you on wonderful adventures, meet many people from all walks of life, visit places you can only dream of and much more. Reading has given me a great deal of pleasure over the years.

However, I thought that writing stories would give me the same benefits, one of which was grief distraction. For hours a day, I lost myself in writing, cutting out the anger, sorrow and 'if only'-s that accompany such sad times.

And it is mainly writing that takes up my time. Writing is not just a matter of sitting down and typing out whatever you want to tell. It all begins with a vague idea, next mentally the plot is outlined, chewed over, will it work doubts, and in my case, all of this anguish is usually just before I go to sleep.

One begins typing, the story grows, then at some point, it stalls. How to go on? Again, just before I sleep ideas formulate. The question is often asked, where do you get your ideas? A few of my answers are, a past experience of myself or friends who, in conversation say something interesting. I often say, 'Hey, can I use that?' Sometimes ideas form just by eavesdropping!

It's finished, a glad and sorry day – what can I write about now? But first, read through the work, correct, tweak and then send it off to the editor. Will she like it? A painful wait, sometimes as long as six months. The manuscript is returned in a draft book form, you read and tweak again, wondering how you missed that in the many times you've already gone through the work. Return the manuscript, it is returned and all as it should be. Read again! Now wait for publication.

The finished book, with cover, is in your hands. But the job is not yet done, time now to go and meet the public, who love to talk to a real author. You give talks and sell at various venues. In between your waits, you write.

Although I have plays, poetry and novels published, to date few of the short stories you will find in this book. Truth to tell, not all of them were submitted and sad to say, many magazines now only publish in-house authors, so I have given up that road.

I am pleased that a number of my articles have been published and are given a second airing in this book. If you are wondering how I know so much, I don't, but I cannot emphasise enough how careful selection of facts and fictions can be found on the Internet has helped.

Short stories are based on a variety of incidents. Some I have experienced or witnessed, some are the result of work set at a writers' group and some just out of the blue and into my head! I have also included a few extracts from my books that I feel fit in.

All creatures great and small

Let's make a start with a conundrum, a task set to write a story with a twist, in one hundred words. Not an easy task!

A Change of Mind

Elsie gazed at the empty armchair at the fireside. Gone forever, she thought, were the long satisfied sighs and the sharing of their favourite foods at the dinner table. No more good night kisses or warm cuddles in bed. She never minded his night-time twitching as he dreamed or his wanderings when he wanted to pee – he was old, alongside her. Now, the quietness of the tidy house and loneliness were unbearable.

Choking back her tears she picked up the phone and said, 'I made a mistake. I want him back.'

'I thought you might,' the vet replied.

The end

The next exercise set was, 'describe someone in a park in two hundred words without using adjectives', or as they say in the trade, 'show, don't tell'.

Rescue

It was a man's voice, a voice that hinted of many years, a voice that penetrated across the park. I turned to see who had called. Behind me someone was brandishing a walking stick and calling. His frame, folded over, convinced me I wouldn't be in any danger if I went to his side.

Again he called, and as I hurried across he leaned on his stick for support. His face told me he had at least seventy years of living. As he took the pipe out of his mouth dripping with spittle, I noticed the veins and spots on his hand. With his pipe, he pointed towards the trees surrounding the park.

'Yonder,' he said. He lifted his cap and with finger nails that hadn't seen a brush for ages, began to scratch his scalp just visible through his hair. I shrugged, not sure what he wanted. 'Me dog, Mrs. She be trapped, I can't reach her.'

To rescue the dog, I had to disentangle her from brambles. When I returned her to him, he patted her and attached a leash to its collar. With tears ready to overspill, he gave me a smile of thanks.

The end

To continue with the dog theme, here is a short story written for reluctant young adult readers.

Duke's Heartbreak

Tonight I resigned from my job. From now on I shall play dumb, refuse to obey and then they will have to retire me. I really loved my work until tonight. Never again do I want to be tested in such a cruel manner.

I don't remember my mother as we were parted when I was a six-weeks-old pup. What I do remember was being tucked inside Mike's zip-up jacket. Mike would have been about fourteen years of age then, 'All arms and legs,' his mother often said. When I came to him, he was shy and lonely, no real friends to speak of and had braces on his teeth which didn't help his shyness. He was so quiet but I knew he loved me. Best of all for me, was his smell, I'd know it anywhere. It was a scent I would go to the ends of the earth for. It was very special to me.

From his smell I could guess his moods. I knew his P.E. days and I knew when he played football. I used to snuffle around his school bag. I could tell by the boots or trainers what the day's sport would be.

I knew when he was happy. Mostly when we were in the woods playing hide and seek. Of course, I always found him quickly, it was that scent of his that gave him away. I knew when he was cross when he came home from school, a door would slam, but he was never cross with me. Sometimes I knew he was upset by the drag of his feet on the floor. I used to prick my ears up and learned it was something to do with teachers and exams.

Mike would carry me about in his jacket when I was small, unzipping it so that my head would poke out. He told everyone my name was Duke. He told them about my family tree and about my special food and our games. My bed was a cardboard box in the kitchen, or so mother thought but it was at the bottom of Mike's bed I liked best. It was warmer and there was his lovely scent.

We went for long walks through fields and woods where I enjoyed a magic of smells. I chased everything and anything that moved. Mike would laugh and call me a 'silly lump' when I returned to him. My tongue would be hanging out and dripping, my tail wagging and my coat wet from the long grass. Sometimes I'd have a swim in the river.

Our parting just a year later was a sad one for me. 'Mike,' said his mother tersely, 'has new friends.' He often came home too late to walk or feed me. Mother would slam my food bowl down on the floor in a temper. My water bowl wasn't filled very often. My coat became matted and I also had a nasty smell about me so Mike's mother said, and made a big fuss about it although I didn't notice it.

Quite often I was able to escape through an open door. Straight away I headed for the woods. The turning point came when I caught my nose on barbed wire. This happened when I belly-crawled under it chasing a fox. It was only a small nick, but bled quite a lot. I made my way home and mother was upset at the sight of my bleeding so much. I was lovingly wrapped in a towel (Mike's scent was on it), and taken to the vet. He said it was only a little scratch and dabbed at it with a wet soft white ball. This had something on it which stung me. I growled and was hard put not to bite him. As it was I showed him my teeth and growled another warning. After a short while, the stinging faded. The vet quickly, but gently, ran his hands over my body and legs and then spoke quite sharply to Mike's mother. I growled another warning. He told her I was a lively and bright dog and that I needed exercise and work. He asked her how I had got to this poor state. After hearing the reasons, he nodded a bit and then said he thought I should go to a local Police Training School.

So began my new life. It meant leaving my beloved Mike. To be honest I loved every moment of being a police dog. To start with, I seemed never to make the right moves for the pointing fingers and stern, firm voices. Soon I learned through warm praise, a rub under the chin and the odd biscuit. I was shown off and showed off at all sorts of shows.

I liked my handler, Tom, but I still ached at times for Mike. Sometimes his scent was faintly in the wind, but of course, my training kept me at Tom's side. My work was catching criminals – whatever that meant. I would have to follow a scent given me by Tom. The scent always had a smell of fear about it. It was quite simple work really.

This evening Tom and I were called out to follow a trail. It was Mike's, mixed with the usual smell of fear. I was so excited. I ran as fast as I could, I was to be with Mike. In no time at all I found him, crouched at the foot of a high wall. I cornered him as my training came to the fore and as Tom wanted. I could not bring myself to hold him in my jaws. Mike put his hand out. I sniffed at the lovely scent that had bonded me to him not so long ago. He put his arms around my neck and lowered his head onto mine and whispered, 'Oh, Duke.' I licked his face and tasted his salty tears.

As Tom led Mike away I knew I had done my job well, almost to the rule book, but in doing so my heart was broken.

The end

Dogs have been in my life for over fifty years. Through the years, members of the family have had rescue dogs, all with their own personalities. The following poem is about our first family dog, Laddie, a rescued mongrel and as independent and defiant as a naughty child. The first day we took him home, he stole a freshly baked family-size apple tart I had left to cool, and he ate the lot! The following poem will give you some idea of his character.

Laddie – A Mongrel

At night a sudden flash of green
Through the darkness thrusts,
By day, amber pools of trust.
Upon the floor you shed
A coat of white, tan and black.
Your odoriferous bed
A raggy sack.

When young your royal ancestors
Pedigree betrayed.
But their instincts with you stayed.
Over commons you go chasing
Rabbits put to flight,
Canine cousins, casual meeting
A rudder greeting, or
Sometimes an unholy fight.

Upturned roots in suburban gardens,
To all house-callers, frantic antics
A pretence of supreme power.
For strangers, a menacing glower.

Padding round on clumsy paws,
Another flowerpot on the floor?
In the street regimental walking,
In the park a game of stalking.

Curled up at last at master's feet,
Running, twitching in your sleep,
A wet-nosed, noisy adorable creature,
Your faithful love
A redeeming feature.

My book, *Towing Path Tales* tells of Bert, a boy who lives on a narrowboat, and this extract is about Nellie, the horse of his childhood.

It was my job to lead Nellie along the towpath, but it wasn't hard as she knew exactly what to do. I knew very well I had to look after Nellie, but have to confess that sometimes I'd let her overtake while I hopped and skipped and chased my shadow or helped myself to blackberries or ripe corn ears. I'd rub the corn between my palms until the husks came off then blow them away and eat the sweet kernels. I fed some to Nellie as she was so well behaved and I sometimes think she understood a small boy needed to run about and play a bit.

In the third book in the series, *A Particular Year*, Bert, now a young man meets up with Nellie who had been sold a few years earlier.

One day I saw a string of horses being led through a market town about twenty-odd miles from ma and pa's. They were mostly old and a few were sickly looking. I knew at once they were for the knacker's yard. Past being able to work, they were on their way to being turned into food or glue, even fertiliser. I stood and watched for a few moments with a saddened heart. Horses are such hardworking faithful animals, their ending didn't seem fair.

As I turned away I thought I saw a horse I knew from the past. The poor creature seemed crippled and had open sores where ropes or an ill-fitting harness had rubbed away her hair and skin. There was mud and thistles in her mane. I stood there for a moment and into my mind flashed a picture of a mare with a gleaming chestnut coat, sharp ears, bright eyes with a harness dressed in glowing brass tokens. I knew straight away the horse in front of me – our Nellie.

'Nellie,' I called out. Wearily her head swung in my direction and then lifted as if seeking me out. I could see such despair and a sadness in her eyes. I cannot begin to tell you how angry I was to see her in this awful state. I rushed up to the fellow in charge.

'That horse,' I pointed to Nellie, 'That horse. Where did you get her?'

He was a surly man. 'What's it to you?' he replied.

'I believe she's mine.' I didn't mean it to be a lie, but at the time I could only think of her as one of the family.

There were gasps from the folks standing around. 'Should be ashamed of yourself,' one woman called out.

'You treat all dumb creatures like that?' another yelled at me.

'Call the police, it shouldn't be allowed.' One woman whacked me across my shoulders with her umbrella, but at the time I felt no pain. I turned to the man.

'Tell me who you got her from?' I demanded.

'None of your business.'

I grabbed his arm and pulled him to a stop. 'Tell me, now or I'll call the police myself. The horse is mine and you've stolen her,' I shouted at him.

'The coppers? You'd call the cops over a mangy horse?' but I could see a visit from the police was not what he wanted.

I shook him. 'I need to know who treated her so badly.'

He pulled himself away from me and said, 'She was tied up to a lamp post. It was obvious she was past working. I reckon someone just left her, so I took her.'

'Then I'm taking her from you,' I told him.

'I'd get a few bob from her at the yard, so 'ow about you buying it back?'

'The police or the horse? Your choice.'

'Charlie,' he called out. 'Cut that old mare loose.' He turned to me. 'She'll be dead in a couple of hours, but don't you come looking for me.'

I had nothing to lead Nellie by and I had a large lump in my throat as she slowly followed me. Then something special happened that brought a smile to my face. First, an apple was thrust into my hand, then a carrot, a bread roll, another apple. It was those same people who had shouted and threatened me and now they were handing me treats for Nellie. After a stop for Nellie to have a long drink at a water trough, we began a long trek home to pa.

The fourth of October is Saint Francis Day who is the patron saint of animals. This has led to a number of churches holding a blessing service for family pets.

October Fourth

The doors opened, the quiet released,
Replaced by a cacophony of noise by beasts.
Furry cats on ample laps,
Perfect pedigrees gently purring.
Old black Toms with thoughts of pairing.
Rabbits, to young chests tightly clasped,
Gently stroking to calm their shaking.
Dogs aplenty, large and small,
Held on leads, tails swishing, wagging,
Delighted by the scents for hunting
And eyeing creatures in the hall.
Fish drifting in crystal bowls,
Fluttering birds, eyes black as coal.
Cavies, intelligent and fascinating,
Bulging cheeks of hamsters munching,
Mice, and rats and gerbils too.
Proud owners, old and young,
Protecting, petting and praises sung.
The church now the local zoo.
All welcomed for St Francis' blessing.

The end

The uniqueness of the seasons

During my happy times in the classroom, at the beginning of each term, I took my class on a two-mile walk to a park. A day in the park, away from the classroom, the children thought. Although there were no swings in the extensive grounds, there was a small tea room. My colleagues and I would have a coffee and the children hot chocolate, ice cream, or whatever. A little playtime and then we set off exploring. My hidden agenda was, of course, to let them see for themselves the changes each season offered. They learned about chlorophyll, photosynthesis and osmosis (English/spelling/science). They picked up leaves, the shape, veins and colour (math, science and art) and through blossoms, berries and nuts, learned about the reproduction of plants.

Nearly always, one or two pupils grumbled about the walk and nothing to do, so here is a poem that captures the essence of what I was aiming for.

The Beholder's Eye

Don't tell me trees are a dismissive green,
Go search the glossy livery green
Of holly, laurel and churchyard yew.
The silvery underside of birch
And the citrus smell of lime
In early Spring.

Don't tell me it's just a leaf,
Look at the serrated edge of beech.
Leaves of the plane, a whole hand span,
Long slender fingers of the willow.
Collectively, a canopy of shade.

Don't tell me just ordinary flowers,
Catkins, pussywillow, ladies' candles,
And clinging witchhazel
Spiders of a yellow flame.
Look again at orchard blossoms,
Pink and red and white.
A confetti shower over Springtime brides.

Don't tell me Autumn walks are boring
When rainbow ticker-tape leaves are falling,
And you kick them crisp and crackling.
Hear the clunk of mahogany conkers,
Promises of jam from quinces, and
Squishy blackberries stain your fingers.

Don't tell me Winter trees are dead,
Stark silhouettes in a steel blue sky,
Nursing secretly, securely, a new verdant dress,
New life tightly wrapped against sparkling ice.

And still through all the changing seasons
The glossy, livery green
Of holly, laurel and churchyard yew.

The end

The following short story was written during one of the years when jobs for school leavers were hard to find, even with good final grades. Springtime is the starting point and the end of summer is more promising for the protagonist.

Something Will Turn Up

'Open it up then Karen,' her mother said anxiously. Karen turned the envelope over; yes, it was from Uxbridge and sported the logo of a well-known local business. Would it be 'yes' or 'no'? Quickly she opened it and read:

'Dear Miss Reynolds,

As stated on our Job Description Sheet we were looking for a candidate with 'A' or 'B' exam results, we were impressed with your recent G.C.S.E. results and your fine voluntary work.'

'Yes, yes,' Karen told herself I've got the job. She read on;

'After much consideration we feel that because you have not yet gained experience in our field of work, we are at present unable to offer you the position advertised'.

The letter went on to wish her well in her search for challenging work. It was over eight months since sixteen-year-old Karen had left school and this was her eleventh unsuccessful application and each rejection was eating away at her confidence. Sensible, would best describe Karen. With her friends, she enjoyed the round of discos and parties, but always home at a reasonable hour. Her fashion sense was modest, dangly earrings and long hair pinned up with a great number of sparkling 'bulldog' grips yes; but no tongue, nose or belly studs. Except for science and French all her G.C.S.E. results were a B grade; the two exceptions were Ds. The problem was that she really didn't know what she wanted to do, and at interviews she never seemed to show enough enthusiasm for the job on offer.

By the look of disappointment on her face, the drooping shoulders and dragging feet, her mother knew the letter's contents. 'Never mind love,' she said as she put her arm around Karen's shoulder, 'something will turn up, you'll see.'

After lunch and still brooding over her disappointment, Karen made her way to the centre where volunteer out-of-work people of all ages were allocated a variety of caring tasks. Her usual jobs were either shopping for an elderly lady, who grumbled at the cost of things and always queried her change despite receipts, or she helped a very harassed young mother with four children under five; she usually took the four-year-old twins to the local park for a couple of hours, treating them to a bag of crisps on the way home. Today Karen was asked if she would visit a blind lady; make her some tea and perhaps read the newspaper to her.

'Who is it?' a cultured voice called in answer to Karen's knock.

A teacher-type voice, Karen thought, and already she felt uneasy, clever people always seem to make her feel inadequate.

'I'm Karen, from the Centre Mrs Boothroyd,' she called out, 'they said they'd phone you.'

'Yes, yes, the door's open, come in. I'm in the room at the back.'

Karen hesitated at the door of an uncluttered room and was surprised to see a well-dressed woman about thirty-five years old with neatly groomed short hair, immaculate make-up and welcoming smile.

'Are you there Karen? Sit down, I'll just make us a cup of tea then you can do something for me,' and she bustled into the kitchen confidently laying out mugs and a plate of biscuits.

'Er, I'm supposed to do that,' Karen volunteered as she followed Mrs Boothroyd into the kitchen and moved towards the fridge for milk. Mrs Boothroyd stopped what she was doing for a moment.

'Just keep still dear, I'll get the job done quicker if I don't bump into you. Milk, sugar?'

Having settled themselves comfortably in the back room, Mrs Boothroyd leaned towards Karen. 'Now,' she said, 'what I want you to do is look carefully into my garden and tell me what you see. It's early March now, and if you start on the left from this window, tell me what you see up to the back fence. Don't leave anything out.'

Karen was surprised at the request and also dismayed. 'Well I'll do my best, but I don't know the names of many plants. Anyway, there's only daffodils there at the moment.'

'Only daffodils!' exclaimed Mrs Boothroyd as she thumped the arm of her chair in mild exasperation. 'Only daffodils! There are many varieties, Karen. Try to describe them, start on the left.'

'Yellow,' said Karen promptly.

'Pale yellow?'

'No, buttercup yellow,' Karen replied.

'Good, good, and what colour is the trumpet? The bell protruding from the yellow petals?'

'Almost white with a narrow orange frill and the leaves are going a little brown at the tips.'

'Ah, frost burn,' Mrs Boothroyd explained. 'Next.'

Peering with more care now, Karen said, 'Sorry Mrs Boothroyd, I missed the violets just a small clump, in front of the daffodils.'

'Oh, bless you. I'd forgotten about them. I could see once you know, so I can "see" what you tell me inside my head. Had a careless accident in the lab. Forgot to pull my goggles down. Large flask exploded on the Bunsen burner. I got a double whammy to my eyes; glass and boiling liquid. Just forgot.'

They sat quietly for a few moments, one remembering the awfulness of her accident, the other just as shocked, remembering the golden rules of the science teacher – goggles and a 'safe flame'. Then quite briskly, Mrs Boothroyd said, 'Let's get on shall we?' Slowly they verbally travelled up the left side of the garden, across the back fence, then along the right side of the garden. Karen doing her best to describe what she saw, and Mrs Boothroyd gently questioning and correcting her. At the end of the afternoon, Karen asked shyly, if she could visit again as she had really enjoyed herself.

A twice weekly visit became a set routine for the next few months. Each month brought new varieties and colours to the garden, and together they smelled and touched them, all the while Mrs Boothroyd passing on tips and information. Karen's interest grew and gradually she could identify many plants. In her science lessons she had been taught flower parts, seed dispersal, water and food intake, chlorophyll and the wonder of photosynthesis but at that time had not really appreciated the intricacies of plant life. Gradually a warm bond of friendship grew between Karen and Mrs Boothroyd, who invited Karen to call her by her first name – Daisy.

'No wonder you like flowers. I think I ought to be Rose or Jasmine,' and they both laughingly agreed on Rose.

Karen's Saturday job in a bakery was boring, and kept her in pocket money but finding a permanent job remained a priority. However, the letters of non-acceptance didn't seem to hurt quite so much. At the end of June, Karen sent off three more letters and waited impatiently for replies. The answers to two of the letters were of 'regrets' and 'too late'. When she opened the third letter and read its contents, she felt she would burst with excitement. Briefly, she outlined its contents to her mother, then rushed off to share the news with Daisy.

'It's here, it's here,' Karen cried, and threw her arms around her friend.

'Listen,

'We are pleased to offer you a three-year Horticulture Course from term beginning twenty-ninth September. Students are expected ...'

'Oh, Daisy, this time last year I was so miserable, now thanks to you, I know what I want to do. Thank you, thank you. I've learned so much from you.'

Hugging Karen back, Daisy said in a very teasing but thoughtful voice, 'How's your Latin dear?'

The end

Haiku

Confetti petal
A gentle snowflake drifts
In a Spring sigh.

A short, gentle ghost story, set in summertime. The names of the characters are made up and loosely based on familiar names: Victoria, Barbara and Edward.

A Timeless Dilemma

Avitoria had watched as the young boy dug furiously beneath the old oak tree. Suddenly his small digging tool struck something hard. He'd found her key. She judged him to be about four years old, the age boys were sent to the fields to scare birds in her time. His clothes were different but he wore a sun hat similar to the wide-brimmed straw ones she was familiar with. She knew he was centuries ahead of her time. It was a hot summer's day and Avitoria smiled as she noticed he was getting red with his exertions.

The key was designed to lift door latches rather than turn locks. It was made of iron and about the length of the child's hand. Excitedly, he picked up the misshapen key.

Avitoria, anxious that it should not be lost, said softly, 'Oh. You clever boy. You've found my key. Please, would you put it back?' She knew he had heard her as he'd turned sharply at the sound of her voice. She watched him hesitate. He can't see me she thought, but he knows I'm here. 'Put my latchlifter back where it belongs under the tree so I can find it later. There's a good boy,' she said.

He turned around slowly shading his eyes with his hand trying to see her in the shadows. He looked towards where she was standing under the oak tree. She could clearly see his freckled face and blue eyes as she imagined her own son might have had. Everything stilled, the air was stifling and there were no sounds. As Avitoria watched, she saw a frown, then uncertainty cross the child's face. Clutching the latch-lifter he ran off, almost tripping as he looked behind him unsure of the sudden change in the atmosphere. She knew there was no point in going after him. She'd never developed any 'materialising' skills, preferring to watch. It was only when the latchlifter was in danger of being moved or lost that she was able to be an onlooker until the key was safe again.

Since leaving the living world, she was still wrestling with the choice of entering heaven to be with her converted Christian family or join her ancestors who were with a God more familiar to her. This was why it was important that she knew always, exactly where the key was. Avitoria fingered the silver brooch pinned onto her fine wool marriage gown, lavishly embroidered by her friend Barita, and sighed. It was entirely her own fault that she was here, stranded, unable to fulfil her second life.

Happiness for Avitoria in the sixth century, was complet-ed the day she received the latchlifter from her husband, Redwald. She knew, as did everybody else, that the latchlifter was no more than a status symbol. After all, latches could quite easily be lifted with the finger. It was given as recogni-tion of her authority over Redwald's household. During their two years of marriage, his mother had organised the house of her rich merchant son. When the matriarch had joined her Ancestors, she took her latchlifter with her. Every woman took her personal latchlifter with her at death as it was said to open the door to the other life where their kin would be waiting for them.

Avitoria had waited patiently for her key, but it was not until her pregnancy was confirmed, that she gained the approval of Redwald and was finally given one. He smiled his consent as she attached it to her chatelaine, and taking her hand, made it clear to everyone that from that moment she was in control of the household.

Although excited by the imminent birth of her baby, and desperately longing for a boy, Avitoria was also anxious. Redwald had made it clear that he wanted a male heir and she wanted so much to please him. Confiding in her friend, she said, 'I know the birthing woman says I'm young and healthy, but ...'

Barita put her arm around her. 'Don't fret yourself. Rest quietly or you'll upset the baby.' She loosened the shawl around her friend, 'There, feeling cooler?' she asked.

Avitoria smiled her thanks and said, 'But many women of my age seem to lose their own lives in childbirth, even the child sometimes.' Reaching for Barita's hand she went on, 'Some women of nineteen have had their third or fourth babies.'

There was a pause, and Barita nodding had said, 'That's true. But you married much later at seventeen, not at fourteen like so many.'

Leaning back in her chair, Avioria stretched out and caressed her growing belly then brightening up, said, 'You're right. Such dreary thoughts. I mustn't upset our son.'

Barita mixed water and ale in a beaker, sweetened it with honey and passed it to Avitoria. Leaning towards Avitoria, she spoke in hushed tones, 'By the way, I saw that man from the new religion today. You know who I mean. Always in black.'

Avitoria stopped sipping her drink and put her finger to her lips. Looking round to make sure they were alone, she whispered, 'Shush. Be careful.' For a moment she said nothing then confided, 'Redwald is very interested in the new religion.' Fidgeting to get comfortable, she went on, 'He has invited that man to dine to question him. He wants to know more about the new God. It frightens me. Anything could happen if our God hears about it.' She lowered her head and twisted her wedding ring round and round her finger, 'I'm afraid for Redwald,' she whispered.

A few days later, the two friends walked to the oak grove as it was time to worship Woden, their God. Avitoria was always happy to be in the peaceful small wood. They had been taught from childhood that Woden had immense power over their lives, he was their God of wisdom. As Barita reminded Avitoria, it was in the grove that she first saw Redwald. Surely it was Woden's wish that they should be together, she'd said. Magical powers and healing gifts were good reasons to worship him. The judging of the good and the bad was another of Woden's attributes. The girls were sure it was he who had punished the woodsman by causing the axe to slice the fellow's arm after he had beaten his wife.

Both girls were afraid of Woden's wrath especially if anyone dared questioned his existence.

Beneath the sacred oak, Barita prayed for her friend to have a safe birthing. Avitoria prayed for her child to be a boy and all that Redwald desired of him. She pleaded with Woden to look kindly on her husband, as he had begun to doubt the old God. 'He is curious and wants to know more and more about the new Christian God, that's all,' she explained. As she turned to go, she noticed a new sapling close by. Woden has given new life she thought, so that there will always be an oak tree here to worship under.

In late summer, Avitoria gave birth to a healthy boy, who was named Lukus by his father. Redwald's delight was tempered three days later when Avitoria began to show signs of fever, the fever that caused death among new mothers. As she began to fail, Redwald implored her to embrace the new faith, swearing the priest had told him of a life in heaven. The priest said special prayers over her imploring his God to heal her, and finally asking Him to accept her into His kingdom, but she hesitated. Woden or Christianity?

As soon as the priest had gone, she asked for her friend. As Barita cooled her with scented water, she rallied and with an effort said, 'I want you to do something for me.'

'Anything to ease your distress dearest,' replied Barita as she continued to bathe Avitoria with a cool sponge.

'I know I shall not be here much longer.' Barita paused in her task and her tears fell silently. 'Don't weep for me now,' Avitoria's voice was filled with understanding. 'Listen, when I am sent to the next world, dress me in my wedding gown, and pin on my silver brooch. Put all my keys, my pearl-handled knife and my sewing purse onto my chatelaine.' She half smiled and went on, 'See that I am dressed and adorned like everyone else who goes into the next world.' She paused, struggling for her breath. 'But ...' Barita put her arm around Avitoria's shoulders to support her better, 'but promise me that you do not add my latchlifter to the burial goods for the afterlife.'

Barita was both startled and shocked by this request. 'But every woman takes her latchlifter. It is the only way you can open the entrance to Woden's Hall.'

'Yes, I know, but supposing Redwald is right after all? That there is only heaven waiting?' They were both silent for a moment. The fear that Woden could overhear them and deny Avitoria a place in his hall was in both their minds. 'Bury the latchlifter under the young oak by Woden's alter. Tell no one of this,' Avitoria whispered. 'If I go to heaven as Redwald is sure I will, then I shall have no use for it.'

'Bury it in the sacred oak grove you say?' Already Barita was fearful of what might happen – to Avitoria as well as herself.

'Yes. Then, if Woden is to be my destiny I will find it easily and make my way there.' She fell back into the cushions, exhausted. 'I think Woden will understand better if the key is safely in the grove. He may even solve the problem for me somehow.' When the time came for her to leave this world, heaven beckoned, Woden beckoned.

All these years later, she was still undecided. The twentieth-century child danced into view. 'Here, just here,' he shouted to his parents who had followed him. 'I found it just here.' He pointed to the recently dug shallow hole. They smiled at each other, delighting in their child's excitement.

'Well now, I think you'd better put it back as the lady wants,' his father said. 'She may be very unhappy if it's missing.' Solemnly the child lowered the key into the hole and covered it with the disturbed earth. 'You know,' the man said turning to his wife, 'there's something magical and serene about this part of the garden.' He looked about him. 'Don't you feel it?' he asked, 'especially around this old oak.'

'You felt it too?' She hesitated for a moment, 'I thought it was just me imagining things.'

He pulled her close to his side and said, 'I knew this place was right for us from the moment I first saw it.'

It was at that same moment, she didn't know how, that Avitoira materialised in front of the boy. He stared at her for a long moment, and overjoyed he called out, 'She's here.' The excited child ran up to her, holding out his hand to be held as children since time began had done to those they trust. She took his hand, feeling his fingers fold around hers. 'I put it back,' he whispered. 'Daddy said you might be sad if I didn't.'

'I saw you. You're such a good little fellow. Thank you.'

At the sound of his voice, the parents turned sharply and saw their child with his hand curled as if holding something and a shy smile on his upturned face.

Avitoria watched as the three of them sauntered back towards their house and smiled. There was no need to make up her mind just yet she thought. Both heaven and Woden could wait a just a little longer now that the latchlifter was safely back in its place.

The end

Haiku

A summer humming
Pollen from spectrum flowers
Happiness is honey.

When my family were children, we spent many happy holidays at the seaside. One time one of the boys went missing from the shoreline, and it was many minutes before we found him happily paddling further along the beach. The next tale, 'Spring Tide', is of a young family's summer holiday. A story where disaster was moments away.

Spring Tide

'You seed him then?' The old man's excited voice penetrated Sally's tumbling thoughts. He sat himself down on the bench beside her and added, 'Aye, you did. I can tell by the look on your face.'

Sally recognised him, he was called Mad Tom by the villagers. Something had happened and it had turned his mind they'd said. She didn't know what but everyone knew him to be gentle and harmless.

He took his pipe out of his mouth and pointed its stem towards the beach. 'There, weren't it?'

The twins shouted out to her from the swings and she glanced towards them then turned back to the old man. 'I'm not sure what you mean,' she answered softly, 'but ...' her hands, wrapped around her plastic beaker holding coffee, were trembling and a tear coursed its way down her cheek.

'Ah! You be a bit upset. Your drink will help settle you.' He stared out to sea as she sipped her coffee, then sighed as he said, ''twas all for the best.'

Sally nodded, unable to speak. What mattered most was that her four-year-old twin girls were safe.

They'd set out quite early that morning and climbed down the hewn-out steps in the cliff face for the small cove below. The beach had been empty and safe for the children to play. The bell ringing in the distance reminded her that probably most people would be in church for the early Sunday service and it was too early for day trippers so they would be on their own for an hour or so. Breakfast was a picnic of orange juice and croissants. She'd changed the children into their costumes, smothered them in lotion and they'd run off to the water's edge to paddle. Sally watched as they started building a sand castle then took out her book. She stretched out on the blanket and waved to them, but the lure of her book beckoned. At the bottom of each page she glanced up at the children – all was well.

That was until she saw a young man in wet cut-off jeans carrying a child under each arm who were struggling and shrieking with laughter. He ran purposefully up the beach passing Sally on his way, the children's bare legs kicking wildly. Her two were now digging out a moat, fiercely concentrating and watching the creeping tide still a good distance away.

Sally returned to her book, 'Debra was afraid to enter the dark room. It was where the Bishop kept his instruments to make his prisoners talk,' she read before raising her head again. Unable to believe her eyes, she watched as the same man she'd seen earlier run past her with the same excited children under his arms.

The man, with a determined look on his face, didn't speak or smile as he passed. There was nothing sinister about him, and yet she felt as if something menacing was about to happen. All seemed so normal, she shrugged, scolding herself for being sensitive, and returned to her book.

'Debra's candle gave only the faintest glow ...' Sally lifted her head from the book and was astonished to see the same man with the children under his arms running past her again. A cold chill came over her, something strange was happening. Things didn't feel right, she felt apprehensive then threatened.

Without another thought, she called to her children. She collected all their belongings and hurried them up the cliff steps to the safety of the playground. On reaching the top and out of breath she halted to look back down on the deserted beach. She watched horrified, it was as if from nowhere, the tide was racing up the beach, covering the place where she had been sitting and smashed into the cliffs sending up a white spray. She felt a hint of it fall on her bare arms and began to tremble as she realised how close they had come to disaster.

'Did ee not know of the Spring tide?' the old man said. 'Plenty of signs about to say it would happen today.' He took a drag on his pipe. 'Locals knowed.' He bent towards her, and she noticed the expectant awe on his face as he said, 'But you saw the lad didn't you?'

Sally nodded. He gave a satisfied sigh, then added, 'Well, folks will think you be as daft as me now.'

She looked at him, puzzled by his remark and he quickly said, 'But us knows better, don't we?'

'I don't understand,' said Sally, watching the girls the whole time.

'Them be your two then? On the beach were they?' Tom asked.

Sally nodded.

He sighed contentedly. 'That's why the boy come then.'

'Tell me, what happened?' she asked.

'Well,' he said, drawing up smoke from his pipe, 'my grandson, Wee Tom we called him, just twenty, courting like lads do.' He stopped to puff on his pipe, the smoke blowing about his whiskered cheeks, then pointed with a misshapen arthritic finger, 'Just over there, mending his father's nets; both fishermen, my son Ben and Wee Tom.'

As Sally watched, he leaned back and closed his eyes. She waited.

'Aye, Wee Tom was mending his nets, when a young mother just about to go down yonder steps to her children, saw the notice,' he turned slowly to Sally, 'the one you missed girl. That one,' his gnarled finger pointed at a clear sign that said, 'Danger, spring tide. Beach reopens at noon.'

'I ... I ... The twins just raced ahead and I, well ...'

Tom patted her forearm, 'It happens. It happens. Kiddies safe now. No need to fret.'

Sally felt herself close to tears again, 'Go on, please, I need to know.'

'That young woman screamed and screamed. Her three children were in the water and already the tide was building up. Everyone thought it was impossible to reach the children before the biggest waves would reach the shore.' He drew frantically on his pipe, twice, then in a broken voice said, 'Then our Tom, Wee Tom ...' He stopped.

Sally slid herself along the bench to be closer to him, and took his hand.

Softly she said, 'I think I can guess the rest.'

Mad Tom, nodded.

'He rushed down to the beach as if the very devil himself was after him. I seed him grab two of the children and run for the steps. The two little 'uns made it, but he went back for the one following him, but being a toddler like ...' He paused, 'Well he couldn't keep up. So Wee Tom went back and ...' He took a furious drag on his pipe, and went on sadly, 'We lost the pair of them.'

Both sat still for a moment, then Tom turned to Sally his eyes searching her face and said, 'So you see, every spring tide I sit here, knowing one day someone would see Wee Tom, I know he is still here. My heart tells me so. And you be the first to see him.' He smiled at her, 'Now tell me, does what you seed this morning make us both mad?'

The end

The following poem was written during one of the more frequent droughts experienced in the U.K. when hose pipes were banned and it was suggested people showered together or share the same bath water!

Dancing in the Street

He danced in the street in his filthy bare feet,
Twirling and twisting like a banshee
Gyrating his desiccate frame,
And we jeered; and made him our game.

He fell to his knees, gave a mumbled cantation,
Then earnestly cried out his wishes.
He spread out his arms and lifted a fist
To the sun in fruitless frustration.

The dread this evoked among the good folk,
Superstition and horror. They desperately prayed.
The rainmaker solemned – no rain today,
And quietly shuffled away.

An early red dawn, just one thread of cloud
No joy in spectators aroused.
The elders peered down the impotent well,
And gazed at the crops with no swell.

But the thread of the cloud grew with the day,
Then a wispy dust swirl was observed.
The clouds billowed and darkened
As wind, torture-howling, unnerved
And to thunder roar villagers harkened.

At last came the rain, fierce and with racket
Accompanied with flashes and crackle,
Overflowing the once empty river,
A gift from the heavens, omega delivered.

Our sorrow, the rainmaker from our village was driven,
But the man was remembered and swiftly forgiven
As the rain jived joyfully around our bare feet
We too, though drenched, danced in the street.

The end

Although spring and summer have an abundance of glorious colour, autumn positively glows with rich hues as well. Some of the flowers seem to survive into the winter months. For me, one of the exciting times of the year is the arrival of seals, seeking safe places to birth their young. From early October, small groups of people on the East Anglian coast begin to search the sea for the first arrivals.

The October Wait

Small groups of people in twos or threes.
Quiet, but excited, they scan the sea.
Dogs told to sit and kept on leads,
They do their best, leashes strained
And frantically pull, deprived of a game.
First the dunes, then sandy beaches
Fringed on the sun-kissed ocean,
Stand patient watchers with gimlet eyes
Unsure, maybe – then the cry,

There! There, with fingers pointing
At bobbing black, sleek heads of seals.

The first to arrive, the first of many.
Winter guests swim peacefully
Along the beach then back again,
Searching for the safest place
To birth and nurse their growing young
Of snow white fur.
The tide washes in the mothers-to-be,
It isn't time, and
With low murmurings, return to the sea.

Waiting, fighting bulls seeking supremacy,
To win the favours of the flirt
Gliding round them in serenity.
Twisting necks, avoid the bites,
They sink then surface in an explosion
of water, pressed together – tight.
Waiting for coupling time in Spring.

Patiently waiting, this October morn,
Those on the shore.
Waiting too, the mothers-to-be
As are the bulls in the restless sea.

The end

Here is a true event in my life during early autumn 1949.

My First Real Date 1949

I winced as I crept into bed and my sister, Joyce, in her usual spiteful way said, 'Serves you right. Dirty cat.'

I didn't care. She can say what she likes but she'll never ever have a day like mine. I smiled to myself in the darkness as I remembered.

I'd got up early; the kitchen was empty and I took off my nightgown and strip-washed in cold water. I dressed in my only frock, plain green cotton that almost matched my eyes.

By half-past eight the rest of the family had come down and my mother waspishly said, 'Well you're dressed early. You can take that dress off for a start. Plenty to do today.'

Breathing deeply, I knew I was answering back when I said, 'I'm meeting Sheila at half-past nine and ...' I hesitated, should I say? Better safe than sorry – so I added, 'and some friends.'

I saw my mother's lips move into a thinness that indicated she was about to lose her temper. I quietly move away from her and see my brothers and sister do likewise. 'Think on young lady,' mother's voice was threatening. 'Your father's already in the garden picking the fruit and you, whether you like it or not, are going to help me with the jam making.'

'But I promised,' I said taking a chance that she might change her mind.

'And you can unpromise,' she snapped back.

Sighing, I asked what I could do to help. I didn't add, 'until I go.'

Mother sniffed and pointed to a basin of black currants that needed destalking and the brown bits rubbed off the bottom. 'Get on with that lot and you can see Sheila later.'

I watched the clock as I worked. It was twenty-five past nine when I downed tools, picked up my purse with the few shillings I earned at Woolworth's and walked out of the door. I could hear mother shrieking after me, but walked on. Dad looked up from his digging and gave a half-hearted wave but said nothing. Today I was meeting Denis. It was my first arranged date.

I'd met other boys in friendly groups. On one occasion one lad had just got his call-up service papers and we all went to the cinema to celebrate. I could tell by the way he held my hand in the dark that he was nervous of leaving home. Then there were the telegram boys, Ted was one. I quite liked him until one day, when we were on our own he said he had something for me. I was curious, naturally. It was a poem. A poem that described how he liked to stand close to me so that he could feel the softness of my breasts. I know I went red and he apologised, but I made it clear I never wanted to see him again.

Alan was seventeen and in the merchant navy, brother of another friend, Margaret. I could never tell her why I stopped seeing him. He was home on leave and we took a walk over the fields then sat on the grass. When he was in New York, he had bought me a lovely little locket with the Statue of Liberty on the front and other bits and pieces.

He said, 'Feel in my top pocket,' and thinking there was another little something for me I put my hand in and drew out a packet of condoms. I jumped up and ran. When he caught up with me, he said, 'I'm sorry, but the lads on the ship said to have them handy, as you were my girl and we'd been out a couple of times. They thought it was time we, we ...'

Well, you can guess, I never saw him again.

Denis had a motorcycle. It seems funny to say, but despite the noise and smell, it was somehow graceful, swooping around other vehicles and leaning slightly left or right on reaching bends in the road. Not only that, but for safety reasons I had to place my arms around this gorgeous boy and I didn't mind one little bit. 'Where are we going?' I shouted in his ear.

'The seaside,' he yelled back. 'Bognor Regis.'

When we arrived, it was the first time I'd ever walked along a beach. Only once had I been to the seaside before. It was during the war and when we, Dad, Gran, Joyce and me arrived, the beach was covered in barbed wire.

On that first date I had, my first ever peach. No such luxuries ever entered our home. I felt its furry skin, smelled its ripeness, then bit into it. Oh! the taste of that first bite and the juice running down my chin.

It was almost eleven o'clock when we returned home. Then out of the darkness loomed my mother.

'Get yourself home now,' she yelled at me. I was mortified as I heard her say, to Denis, 'I don't know what you've been up to, but I tell you now, she's only fifteen.' I saw the look on his face as she grabbed my arm and dragged me up the street. I wished she'd added that I would be sixteen next week.

The washing copper stood just inside the back door along with the copper stick. As we entered the house mother snatched the stick up and whacked me hard across the back and buttocks. I fled to my bed with happy memories of my future husband.

The end

Very little to do with the seasons, but there is a certain age that is sometimes referred to as the autumnal years that I consider to be bonus years. This was a particular favourite of my husband.

Bonus Years

The allotted time is threescore and ten.
Then death's scythe wields the ambushed victim.

From innocent birth to unknowing death,
Dreams, love, laughter, sorrow; until eternal rest.

But there are some who defy that foretold,
Who revel in their secret joys, untold.

They wake and count their blessings day by day,
The smell of rain and new cut hay.

Glad to see again in every extra year,
The seasonal flowers they hold so dear.

Grandchildren happy in their married bliss,
A baby's toothless smile, a toddler's kiss.

They call this extra, thankful time of theirs,
Their welcome, precious, bonus years.

Winter, it is thought by many, is the most miserable time of year. Yes, snow can be slushy even dangerous under foot, but newly fallen snow has its own magic, covering ugliness and dressing the bare branches of trees at the same time. It is the season for celebrations from as far back as pagan and beyond times to present day, religious and cultural customs. These include the lengthening days from mid-December and the promise of the coming of spring.

Searching through my work I can find little to illustrate the season of winter, but include an extract from A Particular Year, the third book in the canal series. The business of transporting goods on the canals was often subjected to the vagaries of the weather. In summer the water used to evaporate until reservoirs were introduced. Winter time in the 1900s was particularly harsh when the boats were held fast in inches deep ice. This in turn, brought much hardship to the boat-dwellers.

1900's Frozen Years

It was the job of the lock keeper to keep breaking any ice that formed behind the gates. Pa said once or twice in the past the ice had been so thick that the canals could not be navigated and everyone had to wait for the thaw. 'And that took weeks,' he'd added.

The keeper came along to the men. 'It's more than I can do,' he said. 'Everything's freezing up again as fast as I be clearing it.' He let out a big sigh. 'I don't reckon there'll be a let up for a few days, but I'll keep at it this night and see what the morrow brings. My shoulders are aching swinging this axe, but I got to keep at it.' I heard his boots heavy on the cobbles as he strode away.

'Best we help the bloke out,' pa suggested. 'We could spare an hour's kip each I reckon.' When he had finished saying this, I saw three men with choppers make their way to the lock gates. They spoke to the lock keeper who was wiping sweat away from his eyes with his forearm. I saw him nod and then point and the men began work immediately. They hacked away and I thought yes, we'll be away in the morning. 'I'll be there in an hour or so,' pa called after them and I heard another voice call out,

'Aye, do yer best so we don't have to work too ... hard.' There was a swear word before 'hard'. Swearing cheerfully was the language of boatmen. The remark caused some light laughter, but most men were anxious about the coming hours.

My sleep that first night was broken by the thump of the various tools chopping away at the ice. I was aroused when pa returned. I half opened my eyes and saw pa nudge Jack. 'Away lad. Get yerself to the lock and give a hand,' he told him. I heard Jack grumbling as he pulled on his boots and pa took his place in the warm bunk.

I was astonished when I woke the next morning. I looked around and could see a sparkling coat of ice on every surface, including the lock gates. Not only were the lock gates well and truly frozen shut, but there was a thick layer of ice round all the boats. The stiffened grass under my feet crackled as I trod on it and the towpath looked like black, dangerous glass. Already behind our boat were another six or seven moored up. I guessed there were probably as many boats moored on the other side of the lock.

Pa poked at the ice with a stout stick. 'Believe it's at least an inch thick already.' He sighed. 'We could be stuck here for days, weeks even.' He turned to the hearth where a low fire just glimmered. 'Ah, well best get that going and treat ourselves to some breakfast.' Then he yelled out, 'Jack, we is starving. Get a move on.'

All day the boat people searched for signs of a thaw, but the cold, freezing conditions continued and everyone was complaining. The folk outside had bright red noses and cheeks and their blue fingers had warm breath blown on them. Some folk stamped their feet, while others clasped their arms tight around their bodies, all doing their best to keep warm.

The next day the canal water was frozen to over three inches thick. The freeze went on relentlessly and after three days pa said, 'Trapped, we are lad.' He shook his head slowly. 'Trapped and for how long I'd like to know?' It was true, our boat, like everyone else's was held fast in the grip of six inches of ice.

The end

Education - Not the three R's

A Career Change

I wasn't exactly miserable. After all I had a good part-time job, I had a comfortable home and a loving family but at forty years of age, I realised I was redundant as a mother. Both my sons were in their teens and life seemed to be the 'hotel' duties of washing, ironing and feeding them. When they were not at home my life felt empty.

All this was to change one afternoon. Our house was the first that children passed when leaving the local primary school opposite. One day, as I was working in the garden at school home-time I saw the first pupil, a little boy, crossing the busy road guided by the school crossing assistant. He was no more than five years old and he rushed up to me glowing with excitement, hopping from foot to foot and grinning from ear to ear.

'Hello,' I said. 'Had a good day?'

'I CAN READ!' he shouted with immense pride and attempted a cartwheel on the pavement. I was the first to know outside of school his great news and he was delirious with happiness. We sat down together on the low garden wall in the warm sunshine, and he read his book with, 'A proper cover and pictures, look,' he said.

He read it from cover to cover, no more than ten words to a page, and the words repeated on every page with a new word added.

The joy of that little lad confirmed for me the wavering decision I'd been thinking of to begin a teachers' training course as a mature student. I was to meet many more little lads like the one who changed my life that day.

Education is not just of the three 'Rs'. No, so much more goes on in and out of the classroom. The following stories are fictitious, but have an element of experience and truth about them.

I begin with a story from the past that I read at a school prize-giving assembly and to present end of term certificates. The certificates were for the children's research work on canals. It was about Bert and his disastrous day at school. Dodging the school board man, whose job it was to ensure all children attended school, was a ruse, especially by boat-dwellers, as they needed to meet orders and get paid.

After reading from the book I noticed a boy who smiled and smiled. I found out he was from the nearby travellers' camp. I realised that some children had been giving him a hard time and he had identified with Bert. At the end of the reading, he punched the air and shouted, 'Yes!'

The School Board Man Visits

The school board man jumped aboard, a pencil and a large book in his hand. He thumbed down a page then tapped the book with his pencil. There was no smile on his face as he looked sternly at my father and his tone was sharp. 'Doesn't tell me here that your children were in school last time you docked.'

Pa scratched his head, I could see him thinking. 'Last time we was here, was roughly six or seven weeks ago.' He scratched behind his ear. 'I'm certain my missus got them washed up proper and sent them off to school.'

I'm not sure if the inspector heard pa mutter, but I did. 'And much good it did them.'

I know for a fact that ma didn't. I know, because I was helping pa to tie up as we docked with a cargo of timber. The rope had slipped from my hands and plopped into the water. Pa boxed my ear for being careless and no one forgets when pa's walloped them. My ear was sore and a bit swollen that it was thought that if anyone saw me in that state, ma and pa might get in trouble for cruelty. Which they ain't by the way, the best any boy could have; so, for sure, we didn't go anywhere near the school.

'Tomorrow morning without fail,' the Inspector said slamming his book shut. 'Failure to do so and I'll make sure the authorities take you to court.'

Ma turned her back on him and dad shrugged and grumbled. 'I'll do me best, but I ain't making any promises.'

The Inspector wagged his pencil at pa and stalked away saying, 'I mean it, Mr, Mr ...?' He gave a little cough, I could see he was embarrassed. He didn't even know our name so he was a fraud pretending to look for us in his register. Ma shut the cabin door in disgust. Dad said something rude like, 'Silly so and so.' Just as the man was about to leave the yard, dad called out.

'Mr, Mr, me eldest lad is thirteen so don't expect him in the morrow.' I was ten and quite small for my age.

However, the Inspector called back, 'All of them, all three without fail.'

Pa grumbled again, but we soon got back to unloading, making jokes with the dockers and drinking tea.

Eight-thirty next morning and the Inspector was hovering about on the towpath. Pa swore, and ma began washing my two sisters. I was already doing one of my chores fetching clean water for drinking and ma's cooking. I was just returning with the heavy cans when the Inspector and myself saw each other at the same time. I put the cans on the towpath quickly and sprinted away, but he was faster. I reckon that's why he got the job. He grabbed the back of my shirt and said, 'Oh, no young fellow. School for you today,' and pulled on my ear with his other hand so that I couldn't escape. Still hanging on to my ear he marched me and the girls to a school just a street away from the canal. It was a very grim looking building and my sister, Emma the youngest and only seven, cried as she was led away with Libby my other sister, through the Girls' Entrance.

At the top of the steps to the Boys' Entrance stood a fearsome chap and the Inspector pushed me towards him. 'This is your teacher, Mr Bush,' he said and he pointed to a long, whippy cane in the teacher's hand. 'Make sure of your manners, young man. No lip or answering back.' He turned to Mr Bush and added, 'You have my permission to strike the boy if he fails in his lessons or if any of the demeanours already mentioned occur.'

Mr Bush nodded, didn't speak but pointed to the yard swarming with many boys and I guessed that was where I should go.

For a while I stood with my back pressed against the school building, overwhelmed by the noise and the hurly burly of many boys chasing and fighting.

Suddenly Mr Bush appeared with a very large brass bell in his hand. He swung this up and down in the air a few times and everybody and sound stopped. He gave a nod and I was astonished to see the boys make a mad dash and line up in rows. I quickly dashed to the end of one line where the boys looked about my size and age. Mr Bush nodded as if satisfied with what he could see, and the first line peeled off into the building followed by the others. When my line entered I went with them and found myself in a classroom with about sixty other lads.

Everything different and difficult. The boys stood beside their desks with attached tip-up seats and were laughing and shouting out insults until Mr Bush entered the room and bellowed, 'Silence,' followed by the same loud voice, 'Sit.' There was a slamming of seats being pulled down and the boys sat with folded arms, except me.

'Boy,' boomed Mr Bush pointing first at me then a vacant seat, 'There, sit.'

I hurried to do as I was bid, but before I could sit the boy on the adjoining seat folded the seat up and I fell to the floor.

There was loud laughter and jeering from the boys, but not from Mr Bush. He loomed over me, 'Stop playing about or you will get a strapping.'

It wasn't my fault and I wanted to explain. 'But Mister ...' I began.

'Shut up, and call me sir.'

Sir? Sir? I wondered. Was he a Lord as well as a teacher? I tried again. 'Please, Sir Mister,' I began.

Again the boys laughed, but it stopped as soon as Mr Bush raised his cane and it whistled through the air as he swiftly brought it down with a bang on his desk.

'Enough,' he shouted and pulled the register towards him. In a monotonous tone he called out names and the owners answered, 'Sir.' He put down his pen and turned to me. My heart was in my boots. 'You, new boy, your name?'

'Bert Smith,' I whispered.

I heard Mr Bush give a moan. 'Not another,' he muttered then thundered out, 'You are Smith seven, seeing as there's six Smiths in the class already.'

A loud bell rang out. 'Stand,' he ordered followed by, 'line up,' and led us all into the main hall for assembly. In ten minutes I learned from the headmaster that there were evil boys in the school as well as the world and that chalk and pencils had been stolen. 'The culprits have been found and will be punished at the end of the day by Mr Bush,' he added. He picked out four boys and dragged them onto the stage. He bent over them and pulled a face. 'How many times have I told all of you, that cleanliness is important and that you should wash daily? These miserable boys have not seen water for a month I declare.' He slapped each of them in turn across the legs with a ruler. 'Tomorrow I shall check to see if you have obeyed my instruction.'

The vicar told us about naked, unwashed savages who were not Christians and he said there were also good pupils in the school. Then the Lord's Prayer was said out loud by everyone except me as I didn't know the words.

The bell went again and we returned to the classroom to begin lessons. Fifty-nine voices repeated over and over again the times tables, but not mine. I didn't know them. If they had talked about dozens and a dozen dozens I would have been fine. Cargoes were counted off in dozens. If the teacher had asked about weight, that would have been easy too. Cargoes of coal, cloth, raw cotton and food were loaded in tons and hundredweights. I sat dumb for a while until the boy sitting at my side, pinched me hard and whispered, 'Say them, water rat.'

I whispered back, 'Don't know them.'

He kicked me under the table, I kicked him back.

'Pretend,' was the urgent reply. 'We'll miss our play if just one of us isn't reciting.' I went along with this idea, just opened and closed my mouth like all the other bored voices. I sighed with relief to hear the bell go again. Mr Bush pointed to a boy.

'Why has the bell been rung?' he asked.

The boy answered, 'Playtime, sir.'

'No, no, no,' barked Mr Bush. I saw his chest swell as he took a deep breath and pointed to another lad. 'You, Smith Two, why?' and I was amazed at the answer.

In one even tone the boy recited, 'To instil obedience, discipline and habits of cleanliness.'

'Correct, to make sure that when you enter your working life you will know when to start and finish; relief times and dinner times. Remember that.' He paused, the playground was filling up with boys and sounds. 'Stand,' he said and pointed to each row in turn to dismiss.

I had a miserable time in the playground. I was pushed and shoved, called names, saying I was dirty, or had lice about my clothes and in my hair. Some boys laughed at my clogs, but I thought I was better off as they were all barefooted.

I decided to look for my sisters. The dividing wall between the girls' and boys' yards was quite high, but I was used to clambering about and I climbed to the top even though I knew I'd be in trouble for this. What a sight met my eyes.

I jumped down into the girls' yard and rushed across to where there was a crowd shouting. There she was my little sister Emma, sobbing with her hands holding on tightly to her ribbon. She was being pushed by one girl and another two were tugging at her hair intent on stealing the ribbon. Mother had spent a good deal of time yesterday evening crocheting fine stitches so that my sisters had pretty ribbons and Emma was determined to keep hers. Libby was trying desperately to pull the attackers away and she in turn was being jostled and thumped. I was so angry, I didn't care any more about the rules saying you mustn't hit girls, and with my fists flying and hitting anyone in my way I finally reached Emma. I kicked one of the girls who promptly yelled and let go of Em.

'Don't want it now,' she sniffed. 'Probably full of fleas and me muvver would 'ave a fit.'

If I had time I would have hit her for that, my ma would have a fit just to hear such words – fleas indeed. I twisted the arm of the other girl behind her back once I had dragged her off Em. 'Leave her alone, now,' I ordered, 'or you will get such a hiding.'

The girl struggled free and laughed, she was a good few inches taller than me. With her hands on her hips she sneered, 'And who is going to make me?'

'I will.'

She laughed again and a good crowd stood around hoping for a fight. 'Come on then. You'll soon be snivelling like this little flea bitten brat.'

It was then I hit her, hit her hard in the stomach. At first she doubled over then straightened up. There was a mean look on her face and I knew I had met my match. Some boys had climbed the wall to see what was happening and egging her on.

'Go on, wallop 'im,'

'Bash the little blighter,'

'Kick 'im, go on, kick 'im,' were the sort of encouragement they were yelling out. Libby and Emma were crying; they could tell I was about to get a hiding. I could see Libby struggling to get away from her captives and I thought to-gether we might have a chance, but she was held fast.

Everything changed suddenly when a whistle was blown. Every girl stood still and I glanced across the yard and saw a short, plump woman hurrying across, her long black skirt almost tripping her up. As she approached the girls stood back to let her pass. When she reached us I could see she was every bit as fearsome as Mr Bush. Her grey hair was twisted into a tight bun at the back of her head, her mouth was a tight thin line and her eyes were slits behind wire-framed spectacles.

Emma crouched behind me.

'What's going on here?' she demanded. She looked first at me then at Em. 'I might have guessed it was something to do with the children off the boat.' She barked at Emma, 'Get up, child.'

Emma, still sobbing but more slowly now, stood in front of her. 'Just look at your apron, child. What have you been doing?'

I looked at Em's apron and besides being covered in dirt, it was torn where the lace hem had been snatched. 'Always trouble, always, when your sort come in.'

'It's not Em's fault,' I shouted at her. 'She was set upon by ...'

The witch, yes she was just like a witch, turned to a girl beside her. 'Fetch Mr Bush, now,' she ordered. 'And you,' she said pointing at me, 'You will be dealt with by him. No one answers back to me. No doubt he will bring his cane with him.'

That was enough, and I turned to Libby. 'Fetch pa, quick,' I told her and she ran off before anyone could stop her. How I prayed pa would get here before Mr Bush. I tried to get back to the wall but was sternly told to, 'Stay just where you are.'

As usual the boys on the wall were jeering, calling out names until the witch turned her attention on them. 'I know all your names,' she said loudly, 'and believe me, if you don't get down now, Mr Bush will hear from me.' There was a quick scuffle as they scrambled back into their yard.

She clapped her hands and it was a signal for the girls to resume their play, although many of them hung about to see what was about to happen as Mr Bush was striding across the yard towards us. His face was twisted in anger and yes, he had his cane with him. I couldn't help it, I began shaking and Emma took my hand; she was as frightened as I was.

'What is it, Miss Morgan?' he snapped. 'There is so little time to enjoy one's tea and biscuits. I really detest being interrupted.'

Miss Morgan seemed to go all to pieces when he spoke. 'I'm so sorry, truly sorry to spoil your break, Mr Bush. I too was summoned away from my drink. I was told there was a boy in the yard. That's not good enough, Mr Bush. I have a duty to my girls. I really cannot tolerate boys for any reason in the girls' yard.' There was a spiteful tone in her voice when she pointed at me, 'Him, Mr Bush. That boy, from the boats. You know as well as I the trouble they cause. He ...' and she listed my misdemeanours, adding some she made up on the way.

He leaned over and gripped my ear and began twisting it and I yelled out with the pain. Em was crying again with her arms around my waist, clinging as if to never let me go.

Suddenly, at last running across the yard was pa. 'Get your hands of my kids,' he yelled. 'Now, I mean it.' Mr Bush let go of my ear after giving it one final twist, and turned to face pa who had rushed up and was out of breath.

'Your children are unruly, bad mannered and ...' but before he could say anything more, pa had grabbed the front of Mr Bush's jacket and pulled him forwards.

'Not true what you say about my kids, never. Their ma sees to that.' I knew by pa's tone that he was in a dangerous mood. 'Even if it were true, that's no excuse for yanking my lad's ear. I tell you now, mister it's only the threat of prison that's keeping me back from thrashing you, but I'll tell you this Mr Schoolmaster, if you ever raise your hand against one of mine again, I'll see you get your comeuppance one dark night.' Pa shook him. 'In fact, if I ever hear of you raising your stick to another child ...'

Some boys had climbed back onto the wall and they cheered loudly at these words. Mr Bush tried to turn and see who they were, but pa was still clutching him to his chest. Pa breathed into Mr Bush's face that had gone a lovely shade of grey, and I was really happy to see he was afraid as pa said, 'You know what I mean?' There was no doubt about it, pa's menacing tone made sure Mr Bush knew it was a serious warning.

Mr B swallowed and replied nervously, 'Yes, yes I do.'

Pa let go of him and turned to Miss Morgan, put his head to one side, gave half a smile and said, 'That means you as well, me dear.'

She was so shocked by his words that her hands fluttered in front of her chalk-white face and I do believe she nearly fainted.

'Come on you two,' pa said cheerfully as he picked Emma up and grabbed my hand, 'Let's go. Be blowed to schooling. Let's see if ma has any blackberry jam, left,' and we departed.

I never went to school again.

The end

Interrupting the school timetable is frustrating for teachers and, as a rule, a delight for the children. One intrusion in nearly every school is the annual photo session.

In the following story, I have met such a teacher as Philip, and listened to tales of woe and romance in the staff room.

As One Door Closes

How dare he! Phil had barged into my classroom – no, he'd crept in, and closed the door quietly.

'Er ...' he began nervously, 'I've brought you a coffee.' He put it down and sat on a child's desk close by. This thoughtfulness was out of character. I looked at him. Unsmiling mouth, immaculate haircut, over clean soft hands. A bit prissy, I thought. We'd been on a couple of outings. Not dates, but there were times when he needed a companion. It suited both of us, and I was flattered to be asked.

He swivelled towards the window to watch the children playing outside. Then he moved swiftly, and banged on the window at some errant child. Slowly he walked back to me. 'Stella,' he said, not looking at me. 'Stella, I wish to terminate our arrangement.' I could see the relief on his face now he'd said his piece.

I was flabbergasted. 'Terminate our arrangement?' I put the mug of coffee down and carelessly splashed two exercise books. 'Terminate is hardly a word I'd use Phillip,' I snapped.

He shifted uneasily. 'You know what I mean,' he muttered.

'We can end or finish it, but terminate sounds rather like assassination to me.' I paused. 'Why?'

'Why? Because it may cause gossip in the staff room.'

'Don't be ridiculous!'

Now he looked straight at me, 'Stella, you're twenty-seven. You must be looking for a husband by now.'

I spluttered almost laughing. Not you, no way I thought. 'Of course, you're so right,' I hoped he noticed the sarcasm in my voice. 'Someone rich naturally and good looking. Someone who doesn't think teaching is all there is to life.'

He blinked his pale blue eyes rapidly and fingered his moustache. I could see I'd rattled him. 'I thought you'd understand. I never intended to upset you.' Almost smugly he added, 'But it proves my point. I can see you're disappointed.'

Seething, I said with as much control as I could muster, 'Thank you Phillip. I quite understand,' and turned back to my marking. I heard the door close as he left. How dare he accuse me of husband hunting!

Our first outing had been to his Golf Club's Annual Ball. The tickets were twenty pounds each he'd explained almost apologetically, and I paid for mine. I'd put up my long auburn hair, and bought a flattering green dress. He collected me exactly on time. There were no compliments. He introduced me as a colleague – I mean, surely he could have said friend at least?

Another time we went to the theatre, buying our own tickets of course. Afterwards we had coffee, going 'dutch'. I'm quite happy with this arrangement as a rule, but when he stated the cost, 'Four pounds and seventy-eight, Stella. That includes the tip,' it niggled me.

It was that same evening that he suggested I invent a boyfriend to mislead the staff. 'Call him Andy,' he'd said. 'Keep them guessing.' Telling my friends about fictitious Andy made me uncomfortable.

As I opened another book to mark, there was a tap at the door. Vaguely annoyed at being interrupted again, and hoping it was a child I could deal with quickly I called, 'Come in.'

It was Mr Davis, the school photographer. I'd forgotten my class was scheduled for their sitting this afternoon. I hated this break from routine. The kids got excited, to-ing and fro-ing between classroom and hall, and some had been known to try to bunk off. Inwardly, I sighed, conjured up a smile and said, 'Mr Davis. Nice to see you again.' I began searching for the timetable hidden somewhere in the clutter on my desk. 'You've come about this afternoon?'

'Hi. Not exactly,' he replied and began foraging in his briefcase. 'Actually, I'd like you to look at these.' He handed me a couple of enlarged photographs. 'Er, I hope that ...'

I gasped in amazement. My anger disappeared in a flash. I was looking at myself; my hair tumbling about my shoulders, a dusting of freckles on my cheekbones, a hint of a smile and my green eyes staring back at me.

'But it's beautiful,' I whispered.

'Aye, beautiful,' he said softly, his brown eyes looking directly into mine. Something inside me turned a somersault, and I felt myself blushing. He leaned over to hand me the second photo. Again the photo was of me, running across the field, my clothes flattened against my body and my hair swinging out behind me.

'You've caught so much movement,' I said.

'Took them both last time I was here. You were chasing one of the kids. I think he was trying to skive off.' His smile was friendly. 'I just pointed my camera and clicked away. Hope you don't mind? Should have got your permission, but ...'

'Good heavens, no. I'm rather flattered actually.'

He pointed to the portrait. 'This one was the winner in a national competition and the other came second in a local one,' he said proudly. He cleared his throat. 'You really like them?'

'They're magnificent,' I replied. Then added hastily, 'You've captured the moments perfectly.'

'I'm pleased with them myself.' A simple pride in his work, I thought, and warmed towards him. 'Well now,' he hesitated, then said, 'the prize money is more than enough for dinner for two.'

The school bell announced the end of the break.

'I was wondering if you'd join me?' There was a pause, 'this evening maybe?'

I didn't hesitate. 'I'd love to,' I answered.

Putting the photos back into his case, he said, 'I'll see you later then and arrange a time. That's a promise.' At the door he turned quickly, and with a grin said, 'My friends call me Andy.'

Later someone asked, 'Doing anything tonight, Stella?'

With heartfelt truth, I answered, 'Andy has suggested a meal out. Somewhere special I believe, he said.' Put that in your pipe and smoke it loser, I thought gleefully as I looked meaningfully at Phillip.

The end

At eleven years of age, a child steps into the next phase of growing-up. One of the first things to happen in September after the eleventh birthday is having to leave the primary school and many friends to begin life in the allotted senior school. For many youngsters the first day can be very daunting. Here is how Rhys, from my book, abridged, *Enormous Responsibilities* reacted and coped with his first day.

Enormous Responsibilities

Everything was enormous. Even the wrought iron gates were higher than any Rhys had ever seen before. Certainly taller than the rec. gates he and his friend, Giddy had climbed and fallen from, since their first day at Infants' School.

It was the first day of his new all-boys school, September nineteen seventy-four. He was eleven years old and, as his father had said, time to grow up and attend the Secondary School.

The day had begun with Rhys putting on his new school uniform, all according to the school's dress code. Long grey trousers, how he longed for the cotton shorts he had worn all the summer months. Black lace-up shoes, grey long socks, a white shirt and a striped blue, black and gold tie.' Emlyn, Rhys's older and married brother, had taught him how to put the right size knot in his tie. Rhys looked in the mirror and was satisfied with his appearance.

As soon as his mother saw him, she tutted. 'Just look at you,' she said.

'What?' He wriggled as she stood in front of him and began fussing.

'That tie for a start,' she said as she undid it and retied it. 'And your shirt needs to be tucked in around the back.'

Rhys gave a sigh and looked across the room to his father who winked back at him. 'You'll learn son. Women are never satisfied,' he called out.

Rhys's mother picked up his new blazer and although she had already brushed it, flicked off, what she thought was a speck of fluff, and replied over her shoulder, 'That's enough from you.'

As he sat down for his breakfast, his mother said, 'I've done your favourite, Rhys. Pancakes with strawberries and ice cream. That will set you up 'til you have your lunch.'

Could he eat it, he wondered? His stomach was turning and churning, he felt sick, he truly had a headache. He knew these excuses would be brushed aside, he'd tried them many, many times before. Was it true, he asked himself, that on the first day, all new pupils had their heads ducked down a lavvy bowl and then someone would flush the toilet? Then you had to go to your class, dripping water from your hair and new clothes and everybody would know? Looking at his breakfast, Rhys felt a little sick again. 'I'm not feeling very well, mam,' he said.

'Once you get the first day over you'll be fine. Emlyn was just the same.'

'But he's older than me.'

Dad laughed, 'He was the same age as you are now when he started the secondary school.'

Giddy, his best friend, who was going to a mixed school, had told him that he would be captured by the bigger boys, have shaving cream plastered over his face, and be shaved. 'Yes, and they would use a cut throat razor and accidentally, on purpose, make sure they cut you until you bleed,' Giddy told him. Rhys wasn't sure if he was being teased, as Giddy had a grin on his face as he related this gruesome information.

Rhys was troubled by these rumours, and went to find out the truth from his gran and granddad. They always sorted out his problems.

'Rubbish.' Granddad had nearly exploded at the very idea and as he repeated, loudly, 'Absolute rubbish,' his false teeth had wavered in his mouth.

'What,' exclaimed his gran, 'You tell me at once, do you hear, if anyone tries any of them larks on you?' Slightly out of breath she added, 'I'll be down that school before you can say Jack Robinson. Everyone will remember Mrs Evans, Rhys's gran, believe me after I've dealt with them.'

Rhys vowed there and then, never to tell her – if it happened.

And yet – Rhys was thrilled, sensing new adventures ahead. Possibly new friends, and hoped that he might meet someone like Giddy, who was full of brainwaves and ideas, many of which had led them into trouble. Giddy's real name was Idris, but he was nicknamed Giddy from the time in Infant, and was always into mischief, making fun and teasing, but at the same time, never told tales. They were both disappointed that they were not going to the same school, but promised to meet up in the rec. to compare the best and worst of their days.

These thoughts were interrupted by his mother saying, 'Eat up, now Rhys, before they get cold. The bus is due in ten minutes, don't want to be late on your first day, do you?'

Well, they did look inviting and he picked up his spoon and tackled the three well-filled pancakes, then smiled with a look of satisfaction.

'Hurry now. Where's your new satchel? Did you pick up your lunch? Have you got your dinner money?' Rhys nodded to all of his mother's fussy questions. Yesterday, his mother had taken him to town to make sure he had the right equipment. Now his satchel was heavy and brimming with new folders, paper pads, pencils, pens and a dictionary.

He arrived at the bus stop with a few minutes to spare. He'd had quite an argument with his mother, who had tried her very best to walk him to the pick-up point in the village to wave him off. 'Everyone will think I'm a cissy, if you're there,' he had protested. He was a little dismayed to see his gran already there, but she was his favourite person, so he tried not to mind. Thankfully, she didn't kiss him or wave him goodbye. Just stood a little back and watched him climb the steps into the bus.

The bus was crowded and noisy, and the bus driver was yelling for everyone to sit down and to be quiet as he drove away to pick up more passengers from the next two villages. These instructions were ignored. Everyone was bigger and taller than Rhys, and wearing the same uniform. As he sat down, he was pushed off the seat. 'That's saved,' a voice from a giant youth informed him. Rhys hesitated before sitting on another empty seat and was shocked to see his fellow passenger, another giant of a boy, secretly smoking.

At each pick-up point, he looked for another obvious, new boy, and was disappointed to find there were none. In a way, he was thankful that the present crowd on the bus ignored him. On the other hand, he would have liked to ask questions, if only someone had spoken to him.

The bus pulled up outside the school and Rhys waited while the rest of the boys shoved each other to be first off and others tumbled or jumped onto the pavement. Rhys was the last to leave, and now he stood before the wrought iron gates that were higher than any he had ever seen before.

Rhys stood in the centre of the two gates, unable to move. It was as if his feet were glued to the ground. He tried to move but only swayed, and afraid he might fall, so stood still. Pupils rushed by, some jolting him, others sauntered past chatting to each other. Still he couldn't move, the crowds thinned, then a couple of latecomers ran past. He heard a bell ring out – the school day had begun and he was still outside. Already he felt he was going to be in trouble.

The avenue to the school building was at least a mile long he thought, and he tried to convince himself that by the time he got to the door, it would be time to go home or at least lunchtime. Somehow he had to make a move and told himself, it's just another school day. But it wasn't. It was a new school and no familiar friends around to talk to. A lump came in his throat and he desperately wanted to go home. Tears filled his eyes as he realised he had arrived by the school bus and the same bus would take him home at the end of the day. Dad had given him emergency money, only to be used for a cab if he missed the school bus home. Briefly, he thought he would use the money now, but knew he would be sent straight back.

Brushing his sleeve across his eyes and swallowing repeatedly, he began walking towards the school building. As he stepped inside, he stood still and heard the familiar school noises. There were hushed teacher tones calling the register, a scraping of chairs and some laughter. There were also well-known smells, mostly polish from the floors and cooking smells. He was in a long corridor with high ceilings and he felt like a dwarf. Suddenly, doors opened from each side and columns of people of different ages and heights marched towards the opposite end from where he was standing. In one group that he spotted, all the pupils appeared to be wearing brand new blazers, and he told himself they were the newcomers.

'You boy.'

Beside Rhys stood a tall, thin, bearded man wearing a long black cloak and a black, flat board on his head and a number of files in his hands.

The end

There is a time in life when people begin to think of their retirement. Sort out the house and garden, hobbies and most importantly pensions. The following is a true event in my life.

I had roughly ten more years of teaching before retirement and I felt I must seek promotion. This would not only help my self-esteem but add money to my final pension. I had a history degree but I enjoyed teaching science at a primary level, nothing too advanced. and found that as I set challenging 'hands-on' work for my pupils, I learned a great deal alongside them.

An advertisement for team head with a knowledge of basic science at a primary school three times the size of the one I was working in, prompted me to apply and I was invited for an interview.

I was ushered into the school library where there were two other candidates, both men and both much younger than myself. Truthfully, I thought I had little chance, just over fifty and female with the wrong degree. I was the last candidate and found the interview panel daunting; the Headmaster, two representatives of the Parents' Association, dignitaries from the Education Department and a local government councillor. I was nervous, made worse by the panel's apparent lack of sympathy as they relentlessly fired off their questions. Then I remembered a piece of advice a colleague had offered. I smiled at the recollection, I felt my shoulders drop and found my voice.

Along with the other candidates we were instructed to return to the library until one of us would be sent for. I was invisible as far as the other two were concerned.

'How did you get on?' asked one.

'Not bad, reckon I did fairly well except one kept asking about the value of computers in future education, and for the life of me I didn't know what the geezer was on about.'

'Well, we'll see. I put up a good interview myself I think. Could use the money.'

One of them turned to me and nodded, 'How about you? Too many men in that lot. Don't really have much time for women in science do they these days?'

'What do you think they were on about? You know computer stuff?'

The other shrugged his shoulders before answering, 'Don't know mate, but I tell you what, I wish they'd hurry up. All my friends are waiting in the pub across the road. Got one lined up for me ready to congratulate me and I'm ready for it.' Then they both laughed.

My blood was boiling, truly they were so sure of themselves, I heard nothing from either about what they could offer the children and thought I wouldn't like one of my children to be taught anything by them.

I turned to the chap moaning about computers, 'Did you not read Mr P's book, just been published but it explains the way forward with computers in the classroom?'

He spluttered, 'No. Oh! No.' He went red, he put his head in his hands, ran his fingers through his hair and strode about the room, muttering, 'Oh, God. Oh, God.'

The other candidate said, 'Hard luck mate. I didn't read it either but that doesn't mean a thing these days.'

I could tell by his demeanour that he was convinced he was now in with a chance. I made up my mind. If either of these two get this job, I shall without a doubt challenge the panel's decision.

At last we heard firm footsteps coming along the corridor and the Head himself appeared. Looking at us all in turn, he put out his hand to shake the hand of one of the men and said, 'Thank you for coming and your time. You may go as soon as you're ready.' Then turning to the other, said exactly the same thing! Beaming at me, he said, 'Would you follow me please,' and back to the panel I went, and was offered the position with lots of congratulations and handshakes.

Whilst having a cup of tea with the group, one said, 'We noticed during your interview that you smiled, then you seemed to get going. Could we ask what made you smile?'

I answered vaguely, 'I can't really remember.' And thought to myself if I tell you, it's goodbye new job. What made me smile?

The advice my colleague had said would always work if one felt stressed out:

'Just remember,' she said, 'they are humans, people just like you with all the same bodily functions. Just picture one of them sitting on the loo with their trousers around their ankles.'

The end

Days at sea

All year round people enjoy being at the seaside. In the first chapter you will have read a seaside holiday story. But being at sea is a very different matter. Seasickness for instance, can put you off for life! I had an uncle who was on the North Sea run during the winter months of the Second World War, and the hardship and suffering was, as he told it, unbearable. At sea, warmer climates also have dangers.

Abandon Ship

Lifeboat adrift, and supplies now gone,
Their enemy, the blazing sun.
Skins burned to desiccation.
Their lives, they knew, were nearly done.

One gave a mumbled incantation,
And earnestly cried out his wishes.
Then spread out his arms, and lifted his fists
To the sun in fruitless frustration.

Dawn breaks, just one thread of cloud
No joy in the hapless crew was aroused.
'til soft gentle rain fell to relieve their thirst.
''Tis salvation,' each mouthed – at first.

Now terrified, black clouds, electric blue light,
Thundered an orchestral tympani.
The wind whipped waves, awesome heights
Then plunged to heart-stopping valleys.

The fountain powered down over their heads,
They clung to each other, each knew the dread
Of every sailor at sea.
That their bodies will lie in the ocean alone,
And their watery graves will never be known.

The end

A short story of a different kind of disaster.

To be with Beth

I bawled out a frantic warning. 'Fire! Fire!' Everyone was galvanised into action. Two rushed to man the antiquated pump, and the rest of us beat at the flames with anything close to hand. I had the inadequate fire blanket, someone a tattered piece of tarpaulin and others used their oilskin jackets. As fast as we thought one outbreak was under control another, fanned by the wind, broke out. Despite everyone's effort, the fire gained a firm hold. Finally, admitting defeat, the skipper radioed for help. Worn out from our exertions, I watched the concerned faces of the others as we pulled on our life jackets and made our way onto the dark, pitching deck lit up by the dancing flames.

'Oi, you,' a voice in the darkness had yelled out just three days ago. 'Looking for a berth?' I hadn't hesitated. Never been to sea in my life but, I thought, I'd be free for a while longer. Not free from guilt or remorse you understand, as it was inevitable that the law would eventually catch up with me.

What I needed at that moment was somewhere for the night. I'd been hitchhiking away from London and my last lift had dropped me off at this small fishing port. I'd heard the heavy engines starting up, shuddering the wooden quayside I was walking along and watched as, one by one, the fishing fleet with their winking red and green lamps made their way out into the heavy swell beyond the sea wall.

The voice yelled out again, 'Well? Yes, or no for God's sake? Can't sail without a cook.'

Cook? I'd be warm and fed working in the kitchen – galley I mentally corrected myself. 'You're on,' I'd shouted back.

'Got your cards?' My heart sank. I shook my head at his words.

'Waiting for them in the post,' I'd lied.

'What the hell ... Forty quid a day, four days, all found. Suit you?'

'You bet,' I'd answered and quickly jumped aboard the last vessel leaving.

'Jim. Jim Smithers,' I said shaking his hand. He grunted a reply and pointed to the hatch.

I'd run away as soon as I realised Beth was dead. It was an accident I swear, but with my record, I'd panicked. For almost all of my twenty-nine years, my temper had been on a short fuse. I'd blown my top for the silliest of reasons and afterwards felt ashamed at my childishness. On police files were two cases of assault I was guilty of in my teenage years. The first was when I'd blacked some guy's eye for criticising one of my friend's footballing skills. I'd also bloodied the nose of another for his disparaging remarks about redheads, mine in particular.

Since knowing Beth I've had better control of myself. That was how we met – my temper. I was arguing with a pal over another girl at a disco. I'd raised my voice and lifted my hand to give him a slap.

'You two. Stop it now. At once, do you hear?' a sharp voice behind me said.

I turned and saw a petite girl with flashing blue eyes, hands on hips, feet apart and a stern look. I felt myself relax and grinned at her nerve taking on two blokes. She smiled back, then laughed, and my heart was captured. She was great at talking me through imagined slights and getting me to laugh at myself.

Of course, it wasn't all roses when we set up a home together. When we bickered, Beth would stomp about the house. I would slam doors and we hollered relentlessly at each other. Eventually one of us would apologise. We'd look at each other, have a fit of giggles and end our differences with a proper loving session. I suppose we were a nightmare for the neighbours. They are sure to condemn me, it probably all sounded a lot worse than it was, so it's a chance for them to get their own back now. What they didn't know was how these flare-ups were quickly over or how sweet the reconciliation.

Beth had worked late that fateful night and I could see by her white face how tired she was. As a teacher, there were often demands for her time after school hours. I chose to ignore the signs. I was tired too, and cold. As I came in I immediately noticed the central heating timer hadn't functioned. She was frantically throwing vegetables and meat into a pot.

'For heaven's sake, not again ...' I began.

'Don't. Just don't start,' she hissed back at me as she dumped peelings into the bin.

'What's up with the heating? I thought you set it this morning. You said you'd see to it,' I said irritably.

She glared at me. 'I did. Not my fault. It needs servi ...'

I shut her up with a groan and in my exasperation pushed her roughly out of the way to search for the instruction booklet. I pushed so hard that she fell, heavily. There was a dull clump as her head hit the stone floor – then silence. Frantically I called her name again and again. I could see her tangled blonde hair was already stained with blood. I knelt down and felt for a pulse. There was none.

My beautiful Beth. Just twenty-six years old. Always bubbling with life and planning our future. We'd talked of a small place in the country, somewhere for me to grow orchids and for her to start a horse-riding school and later, a family. Ambitious I know, but we were determined to get there. Shocked beyond belief I grabbed my coat and wallet and ran, abandoning her crumpled body.

On the small fishing boat, I soon settled into the routine of cooking hearty meals, mainly with the frying pan. Sometimes I was thanked, sometimes I received only surly criticism from the crew. I soon realised their moods fluctuated with the day's catch. A good haul and I was praised, and if small their disappointment became an all-consuming topic of conversation.

There were seven in the crew; the ever watchful skipper, concerned only with the safety of the boat and the welfare of his crew and four tough weather-beaten men, all around the fifty mark. They were constantly calling out instructions, laughing, cursing and hard working all day and sometimes late into the night. There was also a lad of about seventeen called Jack who answered to 'Boy'. He was constantly hosing down the decks to free it of fish waste, a slippery danger to us all, and generally available for every call. And there was myself beset with misery and ashamed I'd run on that dreadful night knowing I'd made the wrong decision.

Towards evening of the third day, and now on our way home, the weather worsened. The wind increased and the sea heaved. The lad, like myself, was apprehensive, his eyes widening each time a wave slid over the bows. Nothing to worry about the experienced crew assured us, at the same time grinning at our discomfort.

As I was cooking the usual fry-up, the boat lurched yet again. The pan slid, the fat spilled and flared up as it splashed onto the gas flame. One of the tea towels drying over the stove slipped, then fell into the hot pan. Its wetness caused the fat to splutter and flare. The flames leapt up almost joyfully to engulf the rest of the towels. Before I knew what was happening, the fire had spread through the cluttered galley and I bawled out that fearful warning, 'Fire! Fire!'

Within fifteen minutes after the skipper's call, a small, too small, helicopter was overhead. The skipper had burned his hands, and two others had inhaled smoke, so they were winched up first. The skipper protested, swearing and insisting he should be last off. The helicopter took nearly twenty minutes to return. It was then I knew time was running out. The helicopter's whirring blades created an unwelcome draught, and it was difficult at first to understand the winch man.

'Three only, sorry mate,' he indicated, making exaggerated signs with his arms to clarify the message.

'No problem,' I shouted back, and pointed to the waiting men. 'Take them. One's only a lad.' I don't think he heard me, but I put my thumbs up to show I had understood. One after the other, I helped strap the exhausted men and Jack, who was shaking with fear, into the lifting harness. Each shook my hand, their gratitude showing in their eyes as they wished me luck and tried to assure me they would see me ashore.

I watched the receding, flashing lights of the helicopter as it flew back towards land. Would it be back in time for me? I felt a loneliness that was beyond endurance. I know I was strong enough to have bullied myself into a place, but what would have been the use? What if I had? I knew the answer – a life without Beth.

The boat was burning fast and I was certain I would not see the helicopter return. I watched the flames flaring as they advanced, devouring everything. As they crept nearer, I felt their intense heat. I realised that in the penetrating cold sea, ten minutes, probably less, would be my survival limit. There was no way out and I was glad and ready. I thought longingly of Beth and wanted to be with her. I like to think she was waiting for me.

The end

An extract from *Don't Shoot the Albatross! Nautical Myths and Superstitions* by Jonathon Eyers, says, 'What a ship was christened, so let her stay'. Long John Silver, in *Treasure Island*, described the grim fates suffered by crews who sailed in a renamed ship. Indeed, at one time it was difficult to find men willing to board a renamed boat.

Was it just a coincidence when Sir Ernest Shackleton sailed to Antarctica 1914 in the *Endurance*, that the voyage ended in disaster? The boat was slowly crushed by the ice but fortunately, no lives were lost. The ship, built in Norway, was named by the builders *Polaris*. Shackleton renamed her *Endurance* to honour his family motto: 'By Endurance We Conquer'.

Many conspiracies surround the sinking of the *Titanic*, another ship to have a tragic ending. One such idea was that R.M.S. *Olympic* was renamed R.M.S. *Titanic* and it was suggested that this possibly was an insurance fraud.

There is one abiding rule, when a ship is renamed, the old name must never be uttered again.

One of the pastimes I and my friends enjoyed was swopping messages, verses etc. in our autograph books. When we left school, junior, senior or college we begged the staff for an entry. Sometimes they only signed it, and if you were lucky a short verse.

One I remember particularly, was 'Your life is like driven snow, be careful how you tread for every step will show'. Another is the plot of the following story.

Rhymes of Childhood

The lightning flashed,
The thunder rolled.
And all the earth was quaking.
The little pig curled up its tail
And ran to save its bacon!

The silly rhyme learned at his mother's knee was going through his head over and over again. At first the needle-like feel of the rain on their badly cracked skins was a relief. All four of them had held their heads skywards to catch the rain in their mouths to relieve their thirst and parched throats. But now it was a relentless, cruel infliction.

Tony, his wife Teresa and their friends, John and Michelle, had been enjoying a sailing holiday. It was Tony's yacht and sailing in the gentle breezes of the Caribbean seas was their idea of heaven. All of them had been sunbathing on deck, the men were in Bermuda shorts and baseball caps; the women wore only the skimpiest of bikinis.

They had waved casually to the crew of a small fishing vessel, and the six men grinned and waved back as they drew alongside. Before the holiday makers were aware of what was happening, the men had boarded the yacht and the four friends were forced, with handguns and machete threats, into an inflatable life raft. These modern-day pirates were ruthless, and had not allowed the four castaways time to collect anything that may have been of use.

The four had been adrift now for nearly two days, and their few emergency supplies in the lifeboat had gone. On this second day, they believed they had seen a smidgen of a coastline. John couldn't remember if the horizon was three or five miles away, but he told the others that if the currents were favourable, they could be on land by nightfall. Their enemy, they thought, was the blazing sun, all of them by now badly dehydrated and burned. Last night it was bone-chilling cold that was their foe.

Then it rained. Salvation, they thought; but by nightfall it was the elements and sea that terrified them. First the wind. They had hoped it would blow them towards the land as it had increased and howled around them. The waves had been whipped into a frightening height so that they were lifted up to a heart-stopping crest, then plunged into a deep trough. The sky, which had quickly darkened with black, rolling clouds obliterating the moon, was lit up by the continuous electric blue of lightning, followed by unbelievably terrifying cracks of incessant thunder.

Now it was night time again, and still the storm had not abated in its ferocity. Tony was gripping his unconscious wife, who had slipped to the bottom of the boat, between his legs that were twisted securely around her body, leaving his hands free to grip the sides of the boat. He heard John begging Michelle to answer him, and when he had no answer, he began screaming obscenities to God.

Tony knew there was no hope. He began his own quiet prayer, murmuring it over and over again until he too sank into merciful unconsciousness. It was another simple rhyme his mother had taught him,

Now I lay me down to sleep,
I pray the Lord,
My soul to keep.

The end

Haiku

Seashore, a winter's day.
Rolling, surging, foaming waves
Crash on the beach.
Shingle shifts, takes a beating.
Broken surge, retreating.

I don't have any more sea stories so thought I'd research further, superstitions and legends of the sea, and there are a great number. One Friday, I was walking along Lowestoft promenade some forty years ago, with an elderly local friend, and coming towards us was a nun. 'Oh, dear,' he said, 'some of the fishermen won't go out today.' The reason given was that if a nun (they called them crows because of their black habits) crossed their path they would have bad luck. This superstition is linked to the death of Christ on Good Friday.

Another superstition relating to women is, if one is aboard she would bring bad luck – that is to say that their presence would distract the men from their work as well as causing the sea to be jealous. In revenge, the sea would summon up a storm with devastating results.

However, it seemed that the gods of the oceans were very keen on naked women (think mermaids). In order to appease these gods, some boats in the past had a carving of the top half of a naked woman on the prow. Or perhaps it was just for naughty sailors.

Naming a ship too, has its share of legend and superstitions. Although, as stated, women were not allowed aboard, nowadays it is always a woman who christens the ship, usually with champagne to bring good luck and prosperity. As far back as 3 B.C. new boats were christened with ox blood and each culture throughout time, spilled blood as an offering to their sea gods, Greek, Poseidon and the Roman God Neptune, in particular. Blood gave way eventually to wine.

In the days of sailing craft, it was considered very unlucky to whistle aboard as it was thought that it would whistle up a storm. Clapping also was considered unlucky, as it might bring on thunder and lightning.

The seamen feared that whales following their vessel would be bad luck, but to have a school of dolphins following was a sign of a good and prosperous voyage.

Today, such superstitions and legends are redundant thanks to science, technology and naval skills.

The workplace

At the tender age of thirteen, I won a scholarship to Hendon College. There were three choices, Nursing, Engineering, boys only in those days, and Commerce. I opted for nursing, but my father said, 'No.' The reason being, that during the war years his youngest sister was nursing and the hardship almost cost her, her life. So the choice was Commerce.

What a gift shorthand and touch typing has turned out to be. Anything from radio talks to university lectures were rapidly taken down in shorthand for further study, and typing up of essays and dissertations were swiftly done. I am beginning this chapter with my first day at college.

Unforgettable First Day

There we sat waiting. Twenty, fourteen-year-old-scholarship girls from all over North West London, waiting for the teacher, not teacher, no, we had to remember tutor. All were properly dressed in brand new uniforms although the berets were strange, conspicuous by their five sided shape that identified us as students of Hendon Technical and Commercial College. Hendon, is famous for two things: The police college and a history of aviation from 1909. So small wonder that the college badge when I was a student had R.A.F. wings prominently incorporated into it.

It was the first day for everyone, and all anxiously looking around the room and not finding one familiar face. One or two coughed nervously, others fiddled about with their new pens and pencils, placing them neatly on the desks in front of them. At least two were in tears. There had been no time really to say more than a 'Hello' or 'Is this Form A/One?' Just the odd shy smile or the scraping of a chair leg as a seat was found.

Then in walked Mrs Roberts our form tutor for two wonderful years, who, by the end of that time was worshipped by all. Quietly spoken, and dressed in a dark suit as if going to the office, tastefully polished pink nails and neat hair, she introduced herself and outlined the curriculum. This, in the main, was shorthand, typewriting, accountancy, French and office etiquette. The latter to include how to dress, deportment and how to handle the office wolf etc.

Picking up her briefcase she said, 'Now girls, follow me,' and led us into a room where resting on each individual desk sat the latest 1940's typewriter. 'Find a place,' she said, 'and that will be your station for an hour a day until you leave.'

Once we had settled she put on a record – a military march with a quick even tempo. When it had finished she asked if we knew the name and after a short silence she told us it was the Radetzky March by Johan Strauss the elder. 'By the end of this term you will all be typing just as quickly and smoothly as that piece of music.' She then told us where to place our fingers on the keyboard, the letters were covered but to begin with we had a paper chart each. 'This is the home line, where your fingers will always return to as you type.' Then slowly she called out 'A S D F J K L.' After a little practice she then told us how to return to the left-hand side of the page by using the protruding lever of the carriage. Then she added G and H, 'Move your index finger to press the key then return it to its home position.' After what seemed a short while, she began calling out the letters at random. 'Now we shall type to music,' she smiled at our unbelieving faces – all of us expecting to type at the speed of the record – and looking round the room I saw faces of bewilderment and panic.

But when it started playing it was slow enough for one to mentally search for the right letter Mrs Roberts was calling out. Then suddenly an extremely low growly voice on the record said 'c a r r i a g e r e t u r n.'

Everyone stopped, shocked, surprised. The music went on but the uncertain atmosphere between the girls was broken. Everyone laughed and laughed, the girls turning towards each other, and from that moment on lifelong friendships were formed.

The end

Mrs Roberts' office etiquette advice included, and we are talking 1940s, never going into the darkroom to develop films with a man! Never walk close to the handrail on stairs if they are the open iron type. It seems men might see up your skirt! No trousers in the office and much more.

More up to date is the following tale set some fifty years later, and not in the least anything like my years in an office.

First Day at the Office

As Angela entered the office, she realised the tight-cropped top, trousers and heavy-soled shoes were a mistake. She sighed, then looked at the three members of staff she would be working with. There were two girls, a couple of years older than herself, dressed discreetly and fashionably. The third person was not unlike her mother and welcomed her with a warm smile.

'Hello Angela,' she said. 'I'm Frances. Come and sit here with me for a bit.' Angela's churning stomach belied her outward confidence. Both the girls looked up and smiled at her.

'*The dragon*, that's what those two call me,' said Frances, and laughed as the girls began half-heartedly to deny it. 'That's Linda, and the other cheeky madam is Kim,' she went on, waving a hand in their direction.

Angela looked at the girls who were once again engrossed in their computer work. She felt a little unsure. Would she fit in she wondered?

Frances broke in on her thoughts. 'It's our job Angela, to see that customers know that they matter. Their first contact is usually with a phone call.' She looked closely at Angela. 'You understand what I'm saying?' Before she turned away to answer a call. Angela watched Linda and Kim. They seemed able to concentrate on their work and chat at the same time.

Frances continued, 'Now,' she said, as she placed headphones onto Angela's head, 'Say nothing, just listen.'

Angela adjusted the headset so that her carefully spiked hair wasn't disturbed.

'Gibbs components Ltd. Good morning. Frances speaking. How may I help you?' she parroted. Angela spluttered.

'God! just like on tele,' she giggled. Quickly Frances switched the caller to 'hold'.

'Never do anything like that again when there is someone on the line,' Frances snapped, as she turned swiftly back to Angela. 'Remember, the company image is very important. Understand?'

Angela looked at the ground and nodded miserably.

When the call was finished, Angela still with her head lowered said, 'I'm really sorry, I forgot.'

Frances sighed, then smiled, 'Well, I don't expect you'll forget again,' and leaning back in her chair said, 'Now you have a try.'

It was mid-afternoon when an irate, flustered man stormed into the office, just as Angela had finished a call. 'Who's the idiot putting all queries through to me?' he demanded. 'I'm bloody busy enough without seven, seven I tell you, simple queries a baby could answer!'

Angela reddened. 'It was me,' she faltered, shocked by the newcomer's tone and bad temper.

Quickly Frances intervened. 'Oh Harry, my fault. I can't have explained everything properly.' She turned to Angela, 'Meet our new girl Harry – this is Angela.'

Angela was dismayed and almost in tears, when quite unexpectedly, Harry put his arm around her, then stroked the back of her neck. 'Poor little girl,' he murmured softly in her ear. 'Did I upset you?' His eyes explored her face then rested on her chest.

Immediately, Angela was uncomfortable, she was aware this was more than sympathy and squirmed away from him.

'Your phone's ringing Harry,' said Frances through compressed lips, and she pushed him away from Angela.

'He's vile, a dirty pervert. I hate him.' Angela shouted after he'd gone. 'How dare he touch me, the toad.' She shuddered at the memory, then burst into tears. Quietly. Frances called to Linda and Kim to take Angela for a tea break. Sympathetically, they escorted her to company's rest room, each doing their best to console her with soothing words.

'He's always trying it on,' explained Linda, as she passed Angela a tissue. 'Just don't give him any chances.'

'Not likely,' retorted Angela dabbing at her eyes, 'next time I'll make him sorry.'

'Don't worry,' said Kim, 'Frances is probably sorting him out right now,' she laughed. 'She really can be a dragon when it suits.'

All three girls got themselves a drink from the machine, and as Angela lifted her beaker, Linda said, 'Love your black nails Angie; I like pink myself, very pretty I think, and goes with anything.' Angela looked at her nails, then at Linda's and Kim's dainty, well-manicured hands. Wrong, wrong again, she acknowledged to herself.

'Tell you what,' Linda continued, 'come to the disco with us on Saturday. Wear your hair like that, and you'll be sensational.'

Angela grinned, as she recognised the implied message.

'Got a boyfriend?' asked Kim, flashing her engagement ring.

'The only fella to make a pass at me lately,' Angela replied as they stood up to go, 'was Harry, and he doesn't count in my book.' All three girls burst into spontaneous laughter, and made their way back to Frances.

The end

When I first began writing, like other authors, I was determined to be ready with answers and dressed to impress. It was a good number of years before such events happened!

The Interview Suit

Everyone knows that dressing in the right outfit for an occasion boosts confidence. When I began writing and fired up with the idea of success, I bought myself a suit, trim but not severe or formal. An ensemble, I felt, perfect to meet my publisher or agent to discuss my work over lunch, maybe not the Waldorf but somewhere as classy, surely? In fact, why not afternoon tea at the Ritz. Those dainty sandwiches minus crusts, scones inches deep with cream and jam, followed by a selection of cakes would be just grand.

Along with the suit I had to have the shoes, with a heel but not too high so that I wouldn't wobble but high enough to prevent me looking dowdy. The right size handbag to carry manuscripts was an essential accessory as was a good fountain pen to sign contracts. Please note, contracts not contract!

With this impeccable outfit the perfect face was of equal importance. Who knows, there could be photo shoots, so I invested in an expensive face cream guaranteed to tighten the skin and even out wrinkles under make-up. Well, I suppose it almost did the trick, I couldn't see it myself but alas time is catching up on me so the wrinkles are definitely more prominent.

Sadly, I'm still waiting for a telephone call for an invitation to lunch, or a meeting with someone from the publishing world. It wouldn't take long to change into my almost haute couture.

I tell myself it will probably be worn out when I do get that special invitation, but hey, when that invitation finally arrives, I might buy a new outfit but you can be sure, I'll be ready.

The end

A short story with a bit of a twist at the end.

All in a Day's Work

It was five o'clock. Charlotte tidied her papers and reached for her coat to go home. Suddenly, someone burst into her office and shouted, 'I want a divorce!'

Startled by this unexpected new client, Charlotte inwardly sighed at the mention of the word divorce and then her professionalism took over. 'Please take a seat.' She watched as the girl, so agitated and unable to keep still, slumped down into the chair that seemed to dwarf her. Charlotte noticed the mascara-streaked tears on her cheeks and the sodden tissue in the girl's hand.

'Shall we start with your name?' she suggested softly.

'I am Daisy Delaway,' the girl announced after checking a sob.

Charlotte wrote it down.

'And your address?' As Charlotte looked at Daisy she could see that she needed a good hair cut.

'6 Abbottsbury Crescent.'

The girl began pleating the hem of her faded top nervously. Charlotte had a fleeting feeling of sympathy for her client, who was too young to be talking of divorce.

'Are you sure this is what you want? We could talk it over if you like.'

But the girl glared at her before answering, 'No. I definitely want a divorce. I never want to see him again.'

'How long have you been with him?'

The young girl eased herself lower into the chair and a small voice muttered something that Charlotte didn't quite hear.

'Is there someone else involved?'

'Yes, my sister!' and a teardrop slid down her cheek, the onset of another hiccupping sob. 'She's always sneaking up to him.' Charlotte looked up and sighed.

'May I call you Daisy?' The girl nodded. 'Now, tell me about your problems and see how best to go forward.' Daisy nodded. Charlotte felt a twinge of pity for this vulnerable and very upset young person and thought, she's just a child really, not understanding the implications of her demands.

'I shall have to make notes, you do realise that don't you?' Daisy shrugged, 'and I have your permission to approach the solicitor who will be acting for the other party?' Daisy shrugged again.

'I need to know the name of the person you want to divorce.'

Daisy scowled. 'His name is Henry Delaway, and ...'

'Also, there are considerable costs involved. One or both of you will have to pay for the services you receive?'

Daisy only muttered, 'Serve him right. I can't move without him interfering.'

'Why do you want a divorce?' Charlotte coaxed.

Daisy shifted nervously in her seat before replying. 'He stopped me going to the new club.' Another tear coursed down Daisy's face.

Charlotte wrote a note and didn't speak for a moment 'Now then,' she said firmly, 'do try to stop crying.'

Already she could see the problem. There was only one new club in town, and it had been visited by the police. Charlotte had heard rumours of a drug dealer hovering around the entrance.

Carefully she asked, 'And what happened?'

Daisy reddened as she shouted, 'I hate him.'

'Calm down please,' Charlotte said sharply.

Daisy glared at her but Charlotte ignored this. Instead, in an authoritative tone she said, 'I need much more evidence please.' For a moment there was a stillness in the room as Charlotte waited for a reply.

Daisy's hands were screwed up tightly in her lap. She took a deep breath, 'You asked for evidence? I'll give you some evidence alright.' She paused, 'I caught my sister kissing him, she had her arms around his neck.' She stared into Charlotte's face. 'Well?' she demanded. There was silence for a moment. 'Do you want to know why?' Charlotte nodded. 'Because he was going to take her out for dinner!' She snorted, 'To a Greek restaurant,' then added, 'I hate foreign food.'

Charlotte asked, 'Anything else?'

'Yes, he's always criticising what I wear.' Charlotte said nothing, she could see that the shorts were really too short and the tee shirt stained. She conceded mentally that perhaps Mr Delaway had a point.

There was a knock on the door. Charlotte saw her husband through the glass window in the door, and called out, 'Won't be long, dear.'

She stood up and put out her hand to Daisy, 'Come on love,' she said, 'let's go and see if we can sort this out with daddy right now shall we?'

The end

A different sort of employment is a career in crime. Here is an extract from *Archie's Children*. Archie, a petty criminal coerces his son, Kevin, into just one more crime to steal a painting. But this time, the job ended badly.

As the house was empty it was agreed around nine would be the best time to carry out the robbery. Kevin decided it would be wiser to take Archie's car. Should, just by chance, anyone see something suspicious and note a car, the robbery would not be traced back to him. His own was after all was said and done, a prestigious model, far too good for the job.

There was an eerie silence about the grounds once the noise of the car engine had died away. The unlit house looked gloomy and uninviting. 'Come on, let's get this over with,' said Kevin as he bent over to tie the lace on his shoe. He patted his pockets, located his leather gloves, not the marigold ones as instructed, and slid his hands inside them, smoothing each finger for a comfortable fit.

With barely a sound Archie prised open the unresisting door with a crowbar, splintering the wood so that it gleamed white in the moonlight. To Kevin, the noise was like a pistol shot and for a moment unnerved him. In an angry whisper he turned on Archie, 'Are you daft or something? Do you want to get us caught, you old fool?'

Archie flashed his new false teeth, 'Nobody about, I told you. Got the place to ourselves. Take as long as we like.' He stood back and pushing Kevin ahead added, 'After you, me lord.'

Kevin stumbled into the hall, Archie followed him and shut the door. They were in a hall lit only by the moon's ghostly, meagre glow filtering through two small windows in the door. Kevin hesitated, trying to allay his unease. There was something not right, the atmosphere held secrets and he had a feeling of danger. Turning back to Archie, he whispered, 'Did you bring a torch? We're not going to risk putting the lights on. They could be seen for miles.'

'Yes,' Archie replied, and promptly turned it on flashing it around the hall they were now standing in.

'Keep it low,' Kevin hissed, 'and keep your voice down.' He glanced nervously along the passage way. Every door each side of the passage painted in mediocre brown, looked forbidding.

'And who's to hear?' retorted Archie. 'I keep telling you we have the place to ourselves.'

Carefully, quietly and methodically they searched each room without success. Each room needed attention, nearly everything was covered in a fine film of dust. Loathe to touch anything but knowing he had to, Kevin kept brushing his hands down his trousers. Archie, wearing rubber gloves, was tempted to help himself to some of the silver objects lying almost carelessly around the room. Archie had an itch over his eyebrow and removed his glove to scratch when he saw a pair of candlesticks. With awe he picked them up. 'Look at this. George the Third I reckon, they were into silver in a big way in them days.' He caressed a salver, put it down then lifted an intricately woven openwork bonbon basket. He gave a low whistle. 'The silver in here is worth a fortune,' he said.

In exasperation Kevin strode across to him and roughly shook his arm.

'Put it down. Forget it. Now.' He heard Archie mumble something under his breath, and taking no notice said, 'I'm going into the next room and if the drawing isn't there, I'm off.' As he left the room Archie spotted a set of spoons and stopped, tempted to take them, but decided against it. Kevin would not be happy, probably cause a scene, even make him take them back.

Utterly exhausted Ethel had fallen asleep and woke to find herself still sitting in the dark and began once again to weep. Suddenly she straightened her back. Had she heard a noise in the hallway? She held her breath for a few seconds and then picked up the walking stick when the soft sound of movement, a shuffle, was repeated. There definitely was someone or something in the hall. Without turning on the lights she crept to the kitchen door, listened and cautiously made her way to the hallway.

Kevin made his way along the passage to the furthest door, tripping slightly over the curled edge of a runner and swore. Archie flashed his torch once more around the room and clicked it off. No more than a few seconds behind Kevin he stepped quietly into the ill-lit passageway. Unable to believe his eyes he was just in time to see someone creeping up behind Kevin and lift a walking stick to strike him. He never knew where the speed came from but in a few quick steps, all in silence, he grabbed the weapon from Ethel's grasp and without a second thought, brought it crashing down on her head. The blow caught her unaware and Archie watched as, with a surprised grunt, her knees buckled and she pitched forward.

Archie moved towards the end of the passageway and turned on the lights. Kevin began to protest, but Archie facing him said calmly, 'It's alright boy, you can be sure there is no one here now. That racket would have brought any other living soul that's around running to see what the racket's about.'

'What's going on?' demanded Kevin. Then he saw the body of a woman at his feet. A sudden feeling of dread came over him, he felt the bile rise in his throat as he looked at Archie still clutching the bloodied walking stick. Seeing his stricken face, Archie quickly dropped the weapon, the crack noise it made as it hit the floor shattered the quietness about them.

'What have you done, you stupid, bloody fool.' Kevin bellowed as he bent over Ethel. 'Christ, if you've killed her, I'm done for proper. How could you be so, so ...?'

'It was her or you – she was about to give you a headache with that stick. Thank your lucky stars I saw her in time.'

Dreading having to feel for a pulse Kevin, hardly able to hold his temper, knelt down beside her and gingerly put his face down to hers. 'She's so still, I reckon you've bloody killed her.'

The end

My mother, for a short time, was a live-in maid for a doctor and his pregnant wife. Mother used to tell me how she had to get up early, light the fires then dust and sweep the rooms to free them of ash before the family came down for breakfast. For years she had my sympathy, until I learned that she just swanned around with a feather duster! Fortunately, she didn't have to face the hazards that the next story reveals.

Giving Notice

At six-thirty in the morning, Molly crept into Lady Catherine Parkes' bedroom and gently pushed her folded letter under her ladyship's bed wrap, draped across the end of the bed. This way, she was certain, that no other member of the household staff could intercept it, read its contents and make sure it was never seen by the intended recipient, Lady Catherine.

Unhappy, often cold, definitely overworked, Molly had made up her mind to go home. A number of things had upset her and although she wanted to run away after the last humiliating occurrence she felt that her employer deserved to know why. Staff were never permitted to approach any family member, indeed it was emphasised that they should at all times be as if invisible to them, so the only alternative as far as Molly was concerned, was a letter.

How though to obtain some paper? Although Molly had access to the study and her ladyship's desk, she felt unable to take just one sheet of notepaper convinced it would be considered stealing. It was earlier in the week when the butcher brought the day's fowls and joints for cook that Molly had some luck when she was instructed to unwrap the meat and put it in the larder. After putting the meat onto separate cold plates it was as she crushed the bloodied paper to throw on the fire that she noticed the outside white sheet was clean and so she folded it carefully and put it in her hessian apron pocket. Later that night in the privacy of her attic room she carefully cut out the best of the paper. It took her three days to complete her letter.

Lady Parkes stretched, yawned, sat up and reached out for her wrap. The white sheets of paper caught her eye as they fluttered to the floor. Puzzled she asked her personal maid to hand them to her. The paper was shiny on one side and rougher on the other and unfolding them carefully she was surprised to see them covered in neat, small handwriting. Intrigued she began reading:

My name is Molly and you have never seen me, not once, although I work in your scullery. It is likely that you only know of me from the housekeeper as 'that girl' or 'girl'. When you find this note no doubt you will immediately believe that I have run away. No my Lady, I have not run away, I have left for my home in south Wales, a home full of love. I was in your employ because my father a scholar, ill and with a large family to feed, thought that I would be better off in a safe household that might be able to offer advancement to a female of fourteen years, especially as he, along with my brothers and sisters, schooled me well in mathematics, Latin and the Classics. Perhaps my father was concerned that his expectations of a good placement were too high, and before I left home, he gave my mother a guinea to sew into my outdoor cloak so that should I find life under a stranger's roof intolerable, I would have the necessary fare to return home. I will have to walk the last five or so miles but by then I shall be happy to be so near to home.

As I leave your household, I am proud to say that I have retained my honour and remained honest in thought and deed. Indeed, the paper this letter is written on, was once the clean wrapping around a butcher's joint so not stolen and the pencil was borrowed from cook. The half day permitted on Sundays I spent in church which kept the Ten Commandments in mind at all times. I will now explain the main reasons for my departure.

I am sorry to tell you that some of those persons known as 'below stairs' are dishonest and disobedient to your wishes. As my family are staunch Chapel people, I cannot be part of such sinfulness. You may be told by the housekeeper that I am disgruntled and lazy. This is not so. It is I who at five-thirty every morning cleans out eleven grates, relay and light the fires for your family's comfort. Already I have burnt my arm on the hot overnight embers. You wake up in a feather bed to a warm room unlike my cold cheerless attic, which is no more than a cupboard, truth to tell. I carry up the three flights of stairs, the buckets of hot water essential for the family's daily morning baths. The buckets are always full to the brim and heavy, and I have lived in fear of scalding myself, especially when the boot boy jumps out of various hiding places to scare me. My daily wash is always in cold water, but I do appreciate the weekly lukewarm bath you permit me.

Do you know I wonder, of the other duties expected of this scullery come parlour maid? Like most of the staff I work fifteen, sometimes sixteen hours a day. My hours are spent scrubbing floors, cleaning silver, preparing vegetables and endless dishwashing. You will be pleased to learn that during the five weeks I have been here, I have not broken one piece of china. However, if I am slow or late the housekeeper beats me. Cook too, slaps me but tells me it's for my own good as she is training me. My parents have never lifted their hand to me, preferring to lead by example and kind words. As I am last to be fed in your kitchen, often I have been hungry as the pots are empty when they reach me, but cook sees that I get a glass of milk and a crust of buttered bread. My family will be shocked to see how thin

I have become. Maybe you think that I am ungrateful for my position but I can honestly say that I was pleased to have an opportunity to learn new skills and thank you for that.

I feel that your Ladyship should be made aware of the dishonesty of some of the staff. As I was the last to retire at night after banking up the fire, I have seen the butler, Mr Bennet, sneak to the cellar and help himself to a bottle of his Lordship's wine and during my short time here this has occurred three times. The last time, Mr Bennet saw me and threatened to get me dismissed if I tell tales on him. I have told you of my being hungry which is unfair, as I have witnessed Mrs Jenkins your trusted housekeeper, hand more than one bag of chops to a gentleman at the back door. I do not know who he is but I think he is the head groom. Also the weekly washer woman always takes home a pie or the remains of the Sunday roast.

You expressly told my father that I was not to have any gentlemen followers, and I add here, that he was scandalised at the very idea, but I assure you my Lady, that two of the under maids creep out late at night to see their young men and I find their saucy remarks embarrassing. There is also much blaspheming by a number of the footmen.

Now I will tell you of the real reason for my leaving. It is unlikely that you know of Thomas, valet to your younger son. My Lady, I have to tell you that I find his constant advances intolerable. Last Sunday when I returned from church Thomas tried to fumble my skirts as well as placing his hands on my upper body. I have managed to avoid being in his company since that time and I am weeping as I relate this to you but trust you will understand my leaving today, 10th April 1905.

Signed by Molly Jones.

Lord Parkes entered the room, sat on his wife's bed and after kissing her, 'Good morning, darling,' looked at her face and asked, 'What's up?'

She thrust the letter at him and said, 'Read that. I don't know whether to laugh or cry at the audacity of the child.'

Slowly he read through the letter, almost laughing, scowling, grunting and smiling in turn, and then visibly shocked at the ending.

'Poor maid,' he said to himself, then turning to Catherine added, 'yes indeed my dear, somewhat audacious but what integrity. Had you any idea that all this goes on with our servants? I certainly didn't.'

She shook her head as she replied, 'I have no reason to go into that domain, as you very well know. I leave it all to the housekeeper.'

Lord Parkes was thoughtful for a moment, then said, 'You had better speak to the women, threaten them with dismissal without a reference, that'll bring them into line. I'll deal likewise with the men.' As an afterthought he added, 'And I'd like to thrash that, what's his name? Yes, Thomas. As it is I'll certainly dismiss him myself, without a reference of course.'

Picking up the letter again, he smiled as he turned to his wife and said, 'You know my dear, it is a pity that this young lady has left us. Would have been an excellent secretary. Such a way with words and her father a scholar too.' Sighing, he added, 'Of course, we could never have her back, the staff below would probably crucify her I shouldn't wonder. But what was the poor child to do?'

Lady Caroline nodded in agreement, 'Yes, it is a pity. I'm sorry she's left without her wages. No more than a few shillings I warrant, but nevertheless ...'

'Send the family a decent hamper that should more than recompense, and when you write, congratulate the father for having such an upright daughter.'

The end

Early spring and in the countryside newborn lambs are leaping and playing or nuzzling their mothers, a delightful scene for the onlooker. It is so easy to forget that this is the busiest and often the most anxious time for shepherds.

Night Vigil with Nell

John sat beside her talking softly. 'You'll be alright girl. Just you wait and see.' There was no answer, just another sigh bordering on a groan. John stroked her stomach gently, telling her it would not be long now. He looked at her fondly, this would be her sixth confinement. All the others went well, so he was confident nothing would go wrong this time. Thoughtfully he remembered the names of the others, Agnes, Annie, Andy, April and August – five girls thankfully. As he watched, Nell turned her head towards him, her eyes wide open as another sigh escaped her. There was nothing more he could do to help her. Again he ran his hand over her stomach, 'Just take your time lass,' he said. Nell seemed then to go into a light sleep, so he took himself outside and lit up a cigarette.

The night sky was clear and he could see way across the valley to the mountains beyond. The village in the valley, some two miles away, was lit by a few feeble street lamps and the odd light in cottage windows. How I love this place he thought to himself, just far away enough to be self-sufficient and near enough to civilisation if needs be. Not tonight though, he'd sent for help as soon as Nell went into what looked like a difficult labour, but a message was sent back with a young lad saying it could be three or four hours before anyone was free. That was at seven o'clock some six hours ago, long past bedtime, but John knew there could be no thought of sleep yet.

Sighing, he went back to Nell, and watched as her legs thrashed and her muscles strained and she panted in desperation. 'Someone will soon be here lass. I don't know how I can help you, but I'll stay with you. You'll not bear this alone.' He began to rub her back methodically, he thought that it seemed to help, it was all he could do. Then nothing – no pushing or groaning, no twitching of legs. Nell seemed relaxed, almost smiling it seemed to him, as she drifted off into sleep. Gradually the warmth and silence seductively lulled John; he fought against it, wanting to be alert when Nell started again, but he lost the sly battle and he too slept deeply as if drugged.

He was awakened quite rudely. Dazed he focused on his youngest daughter, Emma, who was shrieking with delight, 'Wake up dad, Look, look, it's another girl.'

John rubbed his eyes, 'Well, I'll be damned,' he muttered. 'She did it on her own after all.' He gave Nell a 'well done' slap on her rump and then fondled the calf. 'Hello, Audrey,' he said, 'welcome to the flock.'

The end

Of the family

The stories in this chapter are based on events that have happened to members of my family. Naturally, names and places have been changed.

I have also taken advantage of literary license, so a few tales stray a little from the truth. Having said that, I have added a few anecdotes of my childhood, all of which I assure you, are true.

Tucked Away in My Memory

During the second year of World War Two Dad was given a cine projector and two short cartoon films, made by Walt Disney, Mickey Mouse and one of Goofy. Blackout curtains made the kitchen quite dark. The films were thrown up onto a screen i.e. the white enamel splash-back of the cooker. At first, a white bed sheet had been hung to act as the screen, but every little movement about the room created a wisp of a draught and caused the sheet to undulate. We children laughed at the antics of the silent stars from the safety of our beds under the kitchen table. The table was a few feet away from the kitchen dresser which had a pull-down flap with an enamel top for rolling out pastry. The flap would be pulled down so that it touched the table edge then my father put the billiards table over the whole arrangement.

We lived less than a mile away from Northolt Airfield and quite often the films had to stop before the end. Dad was called out on urgent fire watch duty because the flares, seeking the airfield, lit up our houses and as Dad told us, 'We don't want Hitler to know where we live do we kids?' and mutter something like, 'Missed us again you buggers.'

Dad told us endless stories, mostly about men on the moon. Needless to say he was cock-a-hoop when it actually happened in nineteen sixty-nine and I recall the smug look of, 'I told you so,' on his face.

We children, huddled together under the table with our knees under our chins wrapped up in crocheted blankets, hoped Mum would tell our favourite story about her granny.

'My granny,' Mother would say, 'used to live with us when I was a child. I was her favourite. Granny would sit by the range all day long just nursing the children or stirring a pot, but mostly sleeping.

'My mother and father were respected by their neighbours because my dad gave the village a piece of land to build a chapel.' Mother would beam at us, very proud of her Welsh family, then go on. 'They would go to chapel on Sundays and visit two or three evenings a week for a meeting. My big brothers were grown up by now and out at work or courting the girls.'

I remember seeing Mum smile before she continued, 'My granny used to say to me, "See if they've all gone out, girl," and when I said the house was empty,' and here Mum would giggle, 'she used to tell me to turn round and hide my face, but I was a bit artful and peeked round to see what she was up to. I nearly burst trying not to laugh the first time when I saw her pull her long, black skirt up over her knees exposing her gartered stocking tops, then put her hand through the elasticated knickers leg, great big bloomers they were that came down to her knees. Secretly, she pulled out her knotted hankie which held her pension and take out a few pennies.

'"Turn round now, girl," she'd say, and ordered me to go to the chippie which was up the mountain a bit, for some fish and chips for our supper. This would often be straight after our dinner, but we both managed to eat the extra supper I can tell you.'

Looking back on it all now, I can see Mum and Dad did their best to allay our fears in that terrible time. One afternoon, Mother was talking to a couple of neighbours while waiting for me at the garden gate to come home from school. There was a hell of a din in the sky, aeroplanes with the sun glinting on them, screaming in their dives, the rat-tat-tat of their guns and blackened smoke trails.

'Look up there,' old Mr Mason told me excitedly. 'Look up there girlie, that's a real war going on up there.' Twenty minutes or more we stood watching the easily identifiable enemy with their black swastikas and our own fighter pilots with their proud red, white and blue rondels wheeling like silver gulls chasing off the enemy planes. Then it was over, they all flew away. Mr Mason took out his hankie and blew his nose. 'All brave lads,' he muttered, 'someone's son's up there.'

Another time, after three or four nights of bad raids, Dad took all of us to the top of the hill in the early morning.

'Look there,' he said pointing to the east. 'See all that smoke?' We gazed at the distant orange glow veiled with white smoke with plumes of dense black smoke inter-mixed. I can see him now with the baby in his arms, his face showing a shared grief of hundreds, watching the distant City of London burn. There was too, a glimmer of defiance, a look that I was to see time and time again on the faces of the tired friends and neighbours around us. 'That's what the Jerries have done to London, tried to blow it all to smithereens. Well, believe me, they're going to get their comeuppance before long,' said a neighbour shaking his fist at the sky.

At school we were warned not to pick anything up in the roads. We were told that the enemy was dropping toys and other things to attract children and these toys had explo-sives attached to them. Handling them could maim or kill us, the authorities insisted. Boys in particular found this irksome and soon ignored the rules as they searched daily for shrapnel which excited them no end as they discussed the size and swapped pieces of it.

Wartime meant food shortages. The school authorities insisted that every child be given some packed food so that if more than three hours were spent in the air raid shelters, the children could be fed. We also had to take a blanket and Mother crocheted me a very colourful one. These shelters were like long, dark passages dug out in the play-ing field, with a domed roof covered in grass sods. It was always best to be at the tail end of the line of children when we had to go down, that way you ended up nearer the entrance where meagre daylight came in. The hours spent there were never wasted; we learned our times tables and spellings thoroughly.

Only once did the enforced imprisonment sitting on hard backless wooden benches last long enough for the teacher to give permission for us to eat our goodies. I had a cold rabbit pie in its own little, oval, brown dish, it looked lovely and was envied by those sitting close by, but I hated it. I hated the smell and the taste and told my mother so in no uncertain terms and although she said I was lucky to have something to eat, she never gave it to me again. Perhaps the pastry being made with medicinal paraffin oil, an open secret passed on by housewives, had something to do with it. The use of this oil for cooking was soon banned by the Ministry of Food who declared it was unhealthy despite the fact that it was recommended as a laxative.

Mother was proud of what she achieved with dried egg, omelettes stuffed with vegetables made a tasty meal, although Dad wouldn't eat them. We also had pancakes with jam for treats and sometimes scrambled eggs for tea. I liked them all at the time. Fresh eggs were rationed and Dad had the lion's share being the traditional breadwinner. Occasionally, we children were given half a boiled egg with two slices of bread spread with Stork margarine. Breakfast for all of us was usually porridge and fried bread, Dad always had an egg on the bread. There was a plentiful supply of dripping and homemade jam, either of which was spread on bread that I devoured every day after school. At one point, bread became scarce so Mother made what we called 'dampers'. These were made with flour and water and fried in lard and doubled up as bread. They were very tasty.

If a rumour hinting that a delivery of something on ration was promised, queues would form from early morning outside the shop which, because of the shortages, was only open two or three days a week. There was no guarantee that there was enough for everyone, be it butter, sugar, meat or flour, even if the housewife had the necessary coupons. Often I was sent to the shop after school to see if I could get something more, even though Mother had been queuing during the day. Sometimes I heard my mother brag that her children never went hungry, but as my sister said later in life, 'But by God it was boring.'

Civilians during these times were bombarded by various government departments to do their bit for the war effort. Every Monday I would take a sixpenny coin to school and purchase a saving stamp. Sixpences were saved in a little tube with a tin top. When you had forty of these stamps in your savings book you would have a pound. Every week I was determined to get to that amount, but sadly finances and difficulties at home meant that every six weeks or so Mother would cash my little hoard.

Another way of raising funds for the war effort lives on in my memory. There was a street fair held in the local shopping centre for war funds. When I arrived with Dad, I was handed a hammer; he purchased two nails for a penny and handed me one to hammer into a coffin on which was painted a full size picture of Hitler. Mine went in crooked so Dad pulled it out and hammered it relentlessly into Hitler's lower region, somewhere between his legs.

Most Sundays Dad bought the *News of the World* paper, but we children were forbidden to read it. As my parents tutted over the scandals in the paper, I knew something monstrous had happened. Despite their efforts, read them I did. This came about when I used a sheet of newspaper held up to the grate to get a fire started.

Any sort of fuel was scarce and I remember my mother took a saw from the shed and cut down a hawthorn tree at the bottom of the garden. She was very proud of this but it was so green and difficult to burn. To help get a good flame going, a sheet of newspaper with softened Fairy soap on each corner was stuck across the open front of the fireplace which gave way to the chimney, or handheld it in place which was quicker, in order to create a draught. How quickly the fire caught and how dangerous as the paper often flared up in flames; nevertheless, I was able to briefly catch up on some reading whilst holding the paper before it was engulfed.

The end

My war time childhood was divided into two parts. The first was before mother's illness tuberculosis finally caught up with her and she was confined to a sanatorium.

One Friday evening when Dad and I were struggling with the washing my aunt Jennie arrived unexpectedly. My life was about to change as I was told that my sister and I would be staying with my grandparents until Mother was well.

We travelled by train packed with soldiers and I slept most of the way. There were no seats, but we little girls were passed from soldier to soldier. In a hazy sort of way,

I was aware of the soldiers singing, smoking and Jennie flirting and laughing along with them.

In Durham I had my first encounter with the school board officer. On arriving at Gran's, my sister and I, after a sleep and a slice of bread and dripping to tide us over until teatime Gran said, were sent to the rec. to play. Suddenly a stern voice asked, 'Why aren't you in school?'

I replied, 'Cos we've just arrived.'

At once he nodded and said, 'Ah, evacuees. Who you staying with pet?'

I answered, 'My granny, and we're not evacuees.'

'What's your grandmother's name, lass?'

'Mrs Temperley,' I answered, and reminded him again that we were not evacuees.

'Aye, I know her. Well lass, I expect to see you in school tomorrow,' and with that he promptly went to see my grandmother.

When we returned to what was to be our home for the next few years, Gran said, 'Seems you were cheeky to the school board, told him you wasn't evacuees so I can't claim any cash for you, so your da will have to pay for your keep. I was mortified, money, I knew was always tight for my parents.

The end

Nineteen Forty-two

I didn't cry.
You wonder why.

Sanatorium was Mother's home,
To Gran's in Durham, I had gone.
And Dad was left – alone.
I was only nine.
I didn't cry.

Sirens wailed – enemy sighted
Endless falling bombs
Shattering homes every day.
Some of the reasons I was sent away.
I didn't cry.

On Christmas morn,
Above a warming range,
China dogs and chiming clock,
A woollen, bulging stocking hung.
Could this, I wondered be for me.
Gran stood by, gave a nod and smile.

AND I CRIED.

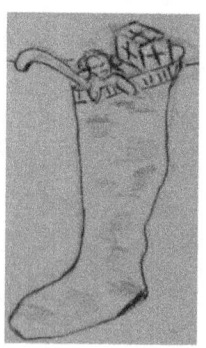

The end

Like most civilians, Gran wanted to do her bit for the war effort, despite having two daughters machining uniforms for service personnel, one a nurse, and another chauffeuring a high official around London, plus a son in the navy. Here is the story of her contribution.

Friday Boys

To me, at that time, they were men. Now I know them to be only just on the threshold of being an adult. I lived with my grandparents in a Durham mining village, in a standard terraced house allotted to miners. Like most homes, the kitchen, a very large one, was the centre of activity. It contained a horse-hair chaise longue on which Granddad, who had suffered a mining leg injury, would stretch out and enjoy his pipe. There was a well-scrubbed table under the window and under the stairs, on a three-legged stool, there was a baby's bath that held water for everyone to wash. The cold water was changed two or three times a day from the only tap fitted at the bottom of the stairs.

Dominating the room was the black-leaded range in front of which was the latest rag mat of many colours that Gran had hooked. The mantel shelf across the top had a fringed, chenille trim. On the shelf was a large striking clock. The range was fed with free coal that miners were entitled to. Never allowed to go out, it kept the whole house warm, there was constant hot water in the side tank and on the other side was the oven. The grange was Gran's domain, she must have been in her late fifties then, she alone did the cooking. In the house were two teenage aunts, one married aunt with a two-year-old child, Gran and Granddad, a teenage uncle, my sister and myself. There was also a cousin, who was the same age as myself and had the same name. This often led to confusion in class and who the infant child blamed for whatever troubled her! The aunts did all the housework and laundering.

Fridays was Gran's baking day. When arriving home from school there was a delicious smell of home baking. Gran stood in the doorway, face flushed and hair escaping from the bun at the back of her head after a full day of cooking. She was a very firm person, some say hard, but always she made sure that the children of the household didn't go without. Indeed, the whole family was very well fed.

But Fridays were different. The floor was covered with clean newspaper. As each batch of baking left the oven, it was placed on the floor. There would be teacakes, fruit loaves, scones, milk rolls, bread in all shapes, and tarts. And we three girls, hungry after the mile and half walk from school, eyed the inviting goodies. But they were not for us. We were given a sixpence to buy a cake from the baker's horse-drawn cart that was along the cobbled back lane. The special baking marathon results were for the evening guests, other mothers' and grans' children.

We were a forty-minute bus ride from Catterick Barracks and every Friday, some of the boys would visit. I thought word had got about of Gran's excellent spread for this influx of young men, but now I believe it was the teenage aunts who were the attraction. One brought a lad home one evening and Gran had generously fed him and told him to bring along a few friends on the following Friday. And so it became a routine and there were never less than six boys and often more. We children were sent to bed early, a ploy to ensure there would be room for the visitors, but we sat on the stairs to watch and listen. As each lad entered, some had to duck, they removed their creased side caps, said, 'Good evening' and if Granddad was not on night shift, shake his hand. Shy, quiet boys, but it was obvious they appreciated the homely welcome. They would read the newspaper, play cards, coaxed to eat up and drink tea or cocoa. As they relaxed, there was laughter and sometimes they began to sing. On leaving they were well-mannered, and thanked Gran, some even giving her a light kiss on the cheek, for her hospitality. We children would see her turn pink, she was obviously pleased.

Now, as an adult, I still have one unanswered question and when visiting Gran in later years, still never found the courage to ask. Where did she get all the ingredients week after week to put on such a spread? Rationing of margarine, butter, cooking fats and suet was reduced to 2 oz per person per week. Also rationed were sugar and eggs. Gran was well-known in the village for her generosity and honesty. Surely she didn't stoop to black market tactics, and anyway, where would she have that sort of money? Perhaps the eggs were from the local farm? Perhaps the neighbours chipped in with a small donation? Did any of the boys have access to the cookhouse and if they had taken anything or bartered for some contribution, Gran would have put a stop to such deviousness. I shall never know, but her warm, homely welcome to those lonely boys justified any hint of irregularities.

As the weeks went by there would be new faces, replacing the boys who had been for a few weeks, and never visited again. Much unpleasant news was kept from children, but now, I realise they were probably doing their compulsory combat training, and sent off to war as soon as possible.

However, there were two boys one of my aunts was keen on. Both wrote to her and should a letter be late from either of them, she would sit by the fire and shed tears. Then the joy when a letter finally arrived. She would sing and dance and cuddle each of us in turn. Later I found out that both the lads survived the war and had asked her to wed them. Both were now adults, handsome and intelligent, and yes she did marry one of them.

The end

The coal mine at the top of a hill, was close enough to Gran's house for us to hear the constant whirring of the water wheel. There was a reservoir where the water was collected, before over spilling down a steep earthenware chute into a brook at the bottom of the hill. My father nearly lost his arm as he swam in the reservoir as there was a dead dog in the water. Dad picked up an infection. Gran of course, did her best to heal this, but when the poison was in red angry streaks almost to the top of Dad's arm, and he was feverish, it was time to call the doctor. Doctors, in those days, had to be paid, so the visit had been put off, nearly too long. Needless to say, he never went swimming in the reservoir again. The more daring boys would slide down the aforementioned water chute.

Alongside the reservoir were pits containing black, warm and malleable tar. This was out of bounds to myself and my cousin. An afternoon modelling tar babies often meant a clout later, as the state of our clothes gave the game away.

In the late 1920s my father, aged twenty-one, decided to leave coal mining and seek work in London. He started work breaking up roads so that pipes could be laid in new housing estates. Here is an extract from my novel, *A Man from the North East* that explains his visit home.

It all began with the smell of frying bacon. Each day he'd heard the chatter of children, a boy and a girl. He was able to confirm this as their toys, a tin doll's pram and cricket stumps lay by the door and the early morning wash was blowing on the line. Every day on reaching the gate a friendly dog rushed up to him and barked out a greeting. Just like the dog next door at home. Today, the dog had escaped, and rushed up to him wagging its tail, its tongue was lolling out and its eyes bright. George knew it wanted to play. He felt his stomach turn. Then a lump rose through his chest and into his throat. He knew he wasn't ill when the moment passed so quickly, but he felt a twinge of sadness.

'Hi fella,' he said as he bent down to pat the dog. 'Got out to see me today have you?' He led the dog back into the garden and closed the gate. Without thinking then feeling foolish, he waved goodbye. He grinned to himself knowing there'd be no waving back.

Later the same day, the desperate feeling suddenly overwhelmed him again. It was when he spotted a matronly woman with her greying hair twisted up behind her head with pins that had worked loose. This time the oddness was accompanied by a pricking sensation of tears under his eyelids. Quickly he got himself under control. Out of the blue, it occurred to him exactly what these crazy feelings were. Homesickness. That's what's wrong with me he realised. A grown lad like me. Succumbing to an age old problem and suffered by most people at some time in their lives. He couldn't believe it. At the end of the day, he'd made up his mind.

'I'm going home,' he said to his boss, then added hastily, 'missing my mam and family.'

One of Dad's greatest pleasures was being with his grandchildren. He always had time for them, sitting them on his knee at the table, and he would cut up his food to share with the child, saying, 'One for you and one for me,' as he popped a morsel into little open mouths. One idea he had, and now copied by his eldest grandson, is described as follows.

Family Tree

Come take a walk in the garden with me,
Said Granddad when I visit for tea.
We stroll down the path,
Watch birds take a bath,
And pick fat pods of green peas.

Then Granddad stops.
Said, 'Look what's grown there!'
And I look and look and I stare.
And I laugh and I laugh,
For what did I see?

Bright colours of red, yellow and green,
All hung from a bough,
And I couldn't think how.
Then Granddad said, 'listen.'
'tis family tradition.

For every child born into the clan,
Be little lady or wee man.
When Grandpa they visit,
And if you don't fidget,
A surprise waits for thee.

And what did I see?
You won't believe me
Magically tied as neat as can be.
I saw – just for me
A lollipop tree.

The end

A little now about my father-in-law, Jack born in 1892. During the First World War he served in the Royal Navy and was sent to Australia to train the Australian Navy personnel. As a boxer, he represented his ship and won a good number of contests.

Returning to the UK he joined the Great Western Railway staff, serving thirty plus years at West Ealing Station.

Here is an account of an event that, at that time, was normal.

Thoughts of Treason

Jack put his bicycle in the shed. It was ten o'clock when he opened his back door after his twelve-hour night shift at the local railway station. He dumped his bait box on the draining board and sat down at the table. Any other day his wife, Connie, would have welcomed him with a kiss and put his breakfast before him. Yes, he smiled to himself, then she would wield the big brown teapot and fill his cup again and again Connie was away caring for her ailing mother and that meant he had to cope, but today he particularly needed her. He was tempted to put his head on his arms and sleep.

The station master had shown him the 'Confidential' message. Everybody working on God's Wonderful Railway as the Great Western Railway was fondly nicknamed, knew the open secret of the message. What it really meant to them all, was over the top spit and polish, meticulous inspections, everyone in their best working uniforms with no sleeved waistcoats on show. The station master would wear his top hat and frock coat, the station foreman-jack, one of three to cover the shift patterns, and the two porters would line up beside him. The gangers, also smartened up, would stand to attention beside the stretch of track they were maintaining. The platforms would be swept again and again, and the already shiny brasses repolished. Tom, his policeman neighbour, would be on duty on the bridge.

The staff had been informed of the reason for all this unwelcome activity – the Royal Train with someone of nobility, perhaps even the sovereign himself, would be passing through the station this afternoon at two-thirty. As if we didn't know, Jack muttered to himself.

Jack set about sponging his best uniform, a job Connie would have done for him and she would have polished his boots, laid out a clean shirt, a clean collar and collar stud as well. All would have been ready when he woke up.

Jack's thoughts were bordering on treason. He had to be back at the station by one-thirty to check the bunting, the brass fitments and the porters in his charge and show Bert, the fourteen-year-old lad porter how to salute. Then the station master would inspect the whole shebang again.

He desperately needed a couple of hours' sleep. That was something else, he thought, Connie would have woken him in good time to have a lathering and a meal. His thoughts now were definitely treasonable. The train was 'only passing through the station, not stopping' for goodness' sake, he told his unconcerned audience, the cat, as he put down a saucer of milk for her.

It was now eleven o'clock, he could snatch a couple of hours, but waking up in good time was going to be a problem. If he lay on his bed he was sure he would sleep too deeply to wake up in time. He could rest on the leather couch, but it creaked with every movement. Bed then, he set the alarm, loosened his tie and braces, tested the alarm and thankfully lay down. He began to drift off to sleep. Surely that was the eleven forty-five whistle, time seemed to be flying. Drifting off again he heard the church clock strike twelve. He groaned and he wished Connie was home. Slowly he relaxed, sighed deeply and was suddenly jerked wide awake by the clatter of Fred's milk churns being taken to the station for the twelve twenty-five. He closed his eyes longing to sleep and then the alarm's strident ring put an end to any hope of a rest.

Jack, along with a full complement of station staff stood to attention and saluted as the Royal Train passed, at high speed, through the station. All that fuss and frustration for a rattle of wheels on rails, a cloud of steam and smoke at high speed and a flash of sunlight on carriage windows. All over in a minute.

As Jack made his weary way home to bed at last, he wondered if it was peaceful in the Tower of London.

The end

A short article, yet to be published.

Charity Shops

Whenever I go out with family, always the girls, nearly all seem to have a fascination with Charity Shops, and I confess so do I. Each has something in mind that they are interested in and seek out.

One of my daughters-in-law makes a beeline for books and always seems to find something that just has that something different in genre and style. Once read, she passes them on to lucky me.

My other daughter-in-law absolutely loves china jugs and has a wonderful collection of styles from many eras. A friend checks out shoes; not only is she interested in style, strappy high heels that she can only wear occasionally, but their colour and material intrigue her. Her husband with poor eyesight heads for the records with his spy glass, the older the record the better pleased he is.

My husband loved drinking glasses, but rarely bought any as most were modern. When we were invited to a number of fancy dress parties, I don't think they are as popular now, in order to dress up we always checked out the charity shops, altered what we bought to suit whatever theme, then after the party took the goods back.

My own forage in charity shops is for earrings of the past, clips or screw only, and I have a number from the 1920s to the 50s which are truly lovely.

The end

Motoring

The delights and disasters of my life with cars.

It was 1947 before I had my first journey in a car. Until then I walked everywhere, firstly because there were no pennies to spare, secondly two miles to school or to a shop wasn't that far Mother said, and lastly there wasn't a bus route. A battered Ford was the company car my father, a Clerk of Works, had for him to visit building sites. For some unknown reason he called it 'Emma'. As a treat some weekends he took the family out for a ride, no more than four or five miles from home, but we all got very excited. There were four children crammed into the back, ages ranging from three to fourteen and Mother, in her felt hat brought out for special occasions, sat beside Dad in the front. One day we ventured as far as Rickmansworth which was approached down a steep hill. It was on the journey back that Dad decided there was no way Emma could possibly get up that hill with a full load, so out we all got and walked whilst Father craftily remained in the car. I'm still puzzled to this day why he felt Emma would die on the upward climb.

During our early marriage we travelled by motorbike and it wasn't until the birth of our first son that we decided to buy a car. A 1933 green Triumph, so battered that the next-door neighbour crossly told us, 'Never park that eyesore outside my house as people might think it's mine and take the Mickey!'

The engine had been a Coventry Climax and was ahead of its time I was told. One evening in mid-winter I was in the front nursing my son and as my husband negotiated a roundabout a back wheel came off. Fortunately, a woman living close by saw what had happened and invited me and baby into her house whilst I let hubby get on with getting the car roadworthy again. No M.O.T.s in those days.

In the 60s with two sons we decided that camping would be fun, so we purchased a van, a grocer's delivery van without windows. The boys were very scathing about this – all their friends had proper cars. They soon changed their minds once we'd packed everything into the back including blown-up mattresses. On the journeys to the sea they were able to romp to their heart's content on the soft flooring. No health and safety monitoring either in those days.

Later we bought a Hillman Husky and although seat belts were not compulsory at the time, we were among the first to fit some. Imagine our shocked surprise when a man asked, 'Do they work?'

We said we hoped never to find out!

I was relieved to read recently that because of a lack of spatial awareness, some women find reversing a car difficult, finally an excuse I can legitimately use. I'll admit to the occasional misjudgement when manoeuvring a car backwards. I was not surprised to see smudges of red paint on the rear wheel arch after a mild confrontation as I (my husband insists) whacked a telephone booth.

Early in 1970, in my own Triumph Herald, I backed into a prefabricated building. A number of these were in the car park to accommodate staff whilst the main office was being refurbished. No damage whatever to the car, but I cracked a panel of the building. The all-male staff rushed to the window on impact, then laughed. The teasing went on for a long time!

To avoid reversing into a difficult space I drive on until I find somewhere easier. I always make a point of reversing into a space in supermarket car parks as my son, who dealt with motoring claims, told me that many claims are a result of two cars opposite each other simultaneously backing then bumping.

Here is a true incident, and was much appreciated by the Yaris Company.

My husband always backed the car out of the garage, but his urgent hospitalisation and illness forced me into the job. We share a driveway, just one car width until it pans out enough for two garages. To reach our garage there is a straight run from the road for about ten yards, then the wall of the house slants acutely to the left. On reaching the end of the house a sharp pull on the steering wheel to the right to straighten up to enter the garage. No problem at all driving in.

It was a long time before I could reverse out confidently; I solved the problem by driving into the garage at the same angle as the house wall. Tricky, but driving out became a doddle. That is until 1991 when we bought a new Toyota Yaris, its dimensions just wider than the old car. I can get the car out of the garage (sometimes having to fold the wing mirror) and then I'm lost. I ask, 'Which way do I turn the wheel?'

He stands in front of me. 'Like this.' He demonstrates. I try to unmuddle the mirror image. He follows me out. I start the engine, then: 'Straighten up.' he yells. 'Watch the wall,' 'Come forward.' 'Start again.'

One day he'd just come out of the shower when I needed to ask THAT question again. The mirror pantomime began.

'No, no,' I protested. 'Sit on the bed and pretend you're driving out of the garage, but the mirror effect confounded me again. 'I'm coming behind you,' I said. He straightened his legs along the bed; I tucked myself behind him tandem fashion. I stretched around him and placed my hands on his. He 'drove out' effortlessly. I understood at once.

Then we caught sight of ourselves in the mirror – me in my puffa jacket, and he in his underpants. We collapsed laughing but who can reverse out now? I change the conversation when my husband suggests buying another car, just in case he chooses one even wider than the Yaris!

The end

I am ending this chapter with a poem, which is self-explanatory.

If Suddenly

Who knows what fate awaits
Those in their evening years.
So, if suddenly my life runs out of time,
Know that I love you.

If cardiac arrest be my means
Of exit from mortality,
A victim of motorway carnage,
Inclement weather or another's rage,

There'll be no time to say
I love you.

If I should be claimed by big 'C'
Or be diseased of brain Alzheimer's or dementia.
Turn not away,
Intrinsic in your heart, be sure
You know I love you.

If from pain I'm never free
And I decide on suicide,
Don't blame or be ashamed of me.
Go on with life and remember
I love you.

The end

To end ...

So, here I come to the last chapter of this treasure trove of my efforts over the last twenty years. I felt unable to place the following into one of the preceding themes, but thought they deserved a reading and might be of interest to you.

Earlier in my writing career I had a contract with a magazine interested in the supernatural. I collected stories from family and friends about their eerie experiences, but it was a short lived contract as the magazine had few sales. What a minefield the unknown is. Some folk were reluctant and embarrassed by their experience, but assured me that what they told me was true.

Here is Philip's tale, I have, of course, changed his name. Philip was about forty-five years old when he told me this, and was twenty-something at the time.

It was a Saturday evening, and I was out, in town some ten miles away, with the lads. I was having a beer, maybe two, and showing off my new car, well not new, but one in good condition and I'd had a bargain.

Gone eleven and time to leave, I'd limited my drinking to two halves, so considered I was able to drive. The drive home was through unlit country lanes, but the moon was full and the car headlights functioning well. Even so, I kept to the speed limit, the cops were, still are, hot on speeding.

Not a soul about, until suddenly an old woman, bent double with a shawl around her head and shoulders stepped out in front of me. I braked, looked back in the mirror and saw ... no one. I got out of the car and ran back to where I thought the accident happened, thinking perhaps she'd rolled into the ditch. There was no sign of a body or living creature. I hung about for a while, hoping I might hear a cry or better still, see her walking towards me. After half an hour I gave up and drove home, even more carefully.

Next morning, I told my mother of the event, and she laughed. 'You've seen Hannah, not many people have seen her. She's a ghost and hangs around in the field beside that road.'

I couldn't believe it and said, 'It was a real person, I saw her, couldn't miss her.' Later that day, I went to the library, searched out some local history books and pamphlets. I was very surprised to read, 'Hannah Smith, 1824-1891 knocked down and died on Benacre Road, by the speeding fast travelling London Coach. A horse also died at the scene.'

The end

A medium once said that I was 'receptive'. 'No thanks,' I replied. Here's why.

Unwelcome Visitor

It was during the early days of my marriage, I was not yet twenty, that one night as my husband was on night shift I had my first 'experience'. I was sound asleep when suddenly the light came on and then off twice rapidly. I began to sweat with fear as I sensed a presence. Then quite gently, with no sound whatsoever, my bed was lifted and then gently lowered. Then all was normal and the fear left me. Was it a nightmare? I thought so. But this happened twice more that week and ended when my husband returned to two weeks of day shifts, during which time the nightmare faded.

Until the night shift came round again. After three nights of this visitation, the routine never varied, one of my senior work colleagues remarked that I was looking dreadful and was there anything wrong. She was a deeply religious person, so I hesitated to tell her of my experiences, but I needed to unburden myself. However, she understood perfectly and told me what to do.

"When it happens again, and it will," she said, 'tell them you are frightened and they must go away. If they are good spirits, they mean you no harm and they will go. If they don't go, tuck your thumbs into the palms of your hands as they may be evil and can enter your soul through your thumbs. If that doesn't work, we will take the next step.'

In the dead of night, it all began again. I know not where I got the courage to say quickly and breathlessly, 'I'm afraid. Go away.'

It worked. I saw a small white misshapen glow at the end of the bed which faded away and that was it. It never happened again. I still hate to think or talk about it even to this day just in case they/it thinks I've opened the door for them to return.

The end

So much for the unexplained mysteries. Now, something a little different, so easy to believe in ghosts when you're nine years old! An extract from book four of Rhys's adventures, *The Sometimes Society*. The two boys were camping out in the local meadow for the night.

During the Night

It was a grunting and snuffling sound that woke Giddy. 'Rhys, Rhys,' he whispered hoarsely.

The reply he received was a gruff, 'Shut up.'

Giddy nudged and poked at Rhys's sleeping bag.

'What? What do you want? Shut up.' Rhys moaned as he tried to get comfortable and go back to his dreams.

'There's somebody outside, trying to get in.'

Suddenly Rhys was wide awake. 'You sure?'

'Listen.' They held their breath as they listened. There was a heavy breathing sound followed by a snort then a faint crackling noise.

'Shall we shout for help, do you think?'

Giddy heard the scared tone in Rhys's voice. 'No one will hear us. Just hope they don't come back.' After a short while there was complete silence, but the boys stayed still and quiet for a long time. Finally, sleep overcame them.

It seemed no time at all when both were woken up by a loud crashing noise outside. The moonlight cast the shadow of something enormous on the tent wall. They could tell it was something alive as the shadow moved. One side of the tent was stretched outwards, then sagged back and they heard an unfamiliar sort of heavy breathing.

'It must be Canrig,' breathed Giddy into Rhys's ear.

'Canrig? What is that?' Rhys whispered back.

'She's a witch, usually lives in Llanberis.' Giddy moved closer to Rhys who could feel his friend trembling.

'No such thing,' he declared trying to reassure his friend. 'They were all burned at the stake millions of years ago.'

'Ruth told me about her.' In the moonlight, Rhys could see his friend's white, scared face.

'She's full of that sort of stuff. You shouldn't take any notice.' Nevertheless, the thing outside moved but had not gone away as they could still hear faint noises.

'Her favourite food ...' Giddy hesitated and choked back his fear. 'They say for her dinner she eats children's brains.'

'Do you think she knows we're in here?' Rhys's voice was very faint and he saw Giddy nod his head.

'Come under my quilt. We can keep each other company and if she tries anything together we should be able to fight her off.' Rhys slid under the inviting warm cover and they put their arms around each other. The strange noises faded away and Giddy stopped trembling. All was quiet again.

'I think she's gone,' Rhys said. Together they slid down under the cover and were soon asleep. Giddy roused once and was comforted by feeling Rhys's leg across his waist and hearing his gentle breathing.

Daylight woke Rhys. 'Hi Giddy,' he shook his friend awake. 'It's morning. Look, the sun's shining.' They grinned at each other, they had survived the night, they were safe.

'Your mam promised us a big breakfast. Come on, let's go.'

'Wait, better be careful. We don't know what's outside.'

Together they crawled to the entrance. Two tousled heads peered out of the tent flap and what a sight met their eyes.

The milk bottle had fallen over and milk had trickled out. Cornflakes were scattered all around and a half eaten loaf had been squashed underfoot. The boys were country lads and the evidence of their fearful night visitors was plain to see. Close by was a curled up hedgehog and hedgehogs make some uncanny noises when they are cross, hungry or facing danger.

Neither spoke, both felt foolish and embarrassed remembering their fears and recognised the simple explanations. Eventually Rhys said pointing to the hedgehog, 'They like milk, Granddad told me.'

Across the field the horse that was in the adjoining field yesterday, was quietly chomping and a pile of dung was close by. Hoof prints were all round the outside and guy ropes dislodged. Pointing at the horse, Giddy said with awe, 'It was him. He nearly frightened me to death.'

The end

This was written when both my husband and myself finally retired and I remember thinking how lucky I was.

Yes, the anguish was there as the house emptied. I missed the music, late night disturbances as the stairs creaked on their return. Sometimes I ached for a hug, and when I looked at their childhood photographs, there was a wrench in my heart. However, I had prepared myself many years earlier, and I feel that particular chapter in my life was less painful than that suffered by others.

I saw my mother crumple as one by one, four of us left home. Eventually my father lost patience with her and gave up trying to appease her. Nearly every time I saw her after my marriage, I had a guilt trip. She complained that no one loved her any more, there were recriminations if phone calls were infrequent, and tearful partings at the end of the monthly visits which, frankly, became a chore. I was determined not to do the same to my children.

When the first of my pregnancies was confirmed, my delighted husband made it clear that until the kids left home, they were to come first in everything, and that we would have time for each other when they go. We had two boys, three years apart. We shared their nurturing, we encouraged their academic ambitions and supported their successes and failures in sport. As they were as different as chalk and cheese, it sometimes proved very interesting.

When the youngest was sixteen, it was pretty obvious that I was soon to be redundant as a mother. It was then that I trained to become a teacher, so that by the time they'd both flown the nest, I was immersed in a second, challenging and rewarding career.

The bonus was as my husband predicted, no measles, no mortgage, shirt laundering down by two thirds, and plenty of fulfilled time for each other.

The following was written as an exercise, 'Being Old,' long before bed-blocking by the elderly and being shipped off to some local home.

In the Geriatric Wards there was, of course, much pain in worn-out joints, frailty because of over-worked hearts, memory lapses and embarrassing accidents, but there was no doubt that the patients were happy. Daily they were encouraged to walk, talk or take part in some sort of challenging therapy. The smallest success, the shaky first steps with a Zimmer frame for example, were greeted with encouragement and smiles and nods of approval.

'Well done Alice, race you tomorrow!'

'I'll be on roller skates tomorrow, so watch out,' was the breathless reply. Then banter would follow from all quarters.

One daily caller was Twinkle, the sleek cat adopted by the hospital staff and patients alike. He brushed himself against old and young legs, and purred his pleasure loudly. When he heard, 'Here puss, here,' he jumped onto the bed and gave himself up to whispered endearments and gentle stroking.

Most evenings there was perhaps a tinge of sadness, when longed-for familiar faces did not appear at visiting time.

'My Billy's working late again,' Elsie informed them all.

'Well, I've got no one tonight either,' answered Mabel, 'I think Pauline said she was on holiday.'

Never any blame, only guessed at excuses. The disappointed soon brightened as the handful of visitors called out cheerful greetings and shared out fruit, chocolate and magazines.

The final pleasure of the day was the news from the Maternity Ward. Sister would telephone just before settling her charges, and relay the number of new babies. They questioned for names and weights, but were content usually to hear 'Six boys, nine girls,' whatever the daily score was. This news always provoked happy discussions of their own babies, until sleep finally quietened the ward.

Advancing years don't come alone, as the saying goes. One such annoying, but manageable, aspect is being hard of hearing, a condition that is equally annoying to those trying to speak to you. Here is a poem, written in frustration.

When Hearing Fades

I'm lost in a confusion of consonants,
And search for vowels to make sense,
And so often I'm wrong – it's depressing.

Do I hear your impatience you wonder?
Your tone asking got your aids?

The lift of your shoulders, closing of eyes,
And you, not seeing my pain.
Aids I have yes,
Some sounds, still a guess
Like creaking and squeaking
Sibilant hissing,

I don't hear when you call.
I can't hear, I tell all.
I'll shout, they thoughtlessly reply.
I say, look at me – I read lips.

They smile, start with exaggeration,
That too, is aggravation.
To their mouths, stray hands flutter
Or turn away, without knowing
I no longer see, hear only mutters.

Yes, I wear aids, gladly.
And hear playground laughter,
And groans, a football disaster.
The sighing of leaves
When the wind passes through.
Night foxes that bark, heard too.
The singing of kettles,
The tick of the clock,
Backfiring cars deliver a shock.

Senses, sight, smell, touch and taste
Still working and playing their part.
As is my heart.
So patience, I beg if dense I appear.
It's simply because I no longer can hear.

The end

I expect some of my readers are able to identify with these feelings.

Now for something entirely different.

Retribution

Steve was tired. When he planned his walking holiday, he hadn't realised that, once on the moors, the chance of finding a night's accommodation would be so difficult. When, he saw a sign B&B he sighed with relief, hastened his step, and was soon at the door of the lonely, run-down inn.

Frank, the landlord, made him welcome and when Steve paid for his night's lodging in advance, he enviously eyed the bulging wallet. 'On your own?' he asked. 'No girlfriend, family?' Steve's reply was as he hoped.

'That's right. On my own.' He smiled. 'No one. There is a girl, but ...' He trailed off. 'I've got a brother somewhere in Australia, and that's about it,' he'd added.

Frank was satisfied. A loner, he thought. A lethal drink, hide the body later, somewhere desolate on the moor. No problem.

At bedtime, he nodded to Steve, and said, 'Left you out a hot drink. See you in the morning. Breakfast eight-thirty. Suit you?'

Steve nodded, and said, 'Thanks, much appreciated. Goodnight.'

Since boyhood, Steve had always been mesmerised by fire. He looked about the kitchen, fires nearly always started in kitchens. He settled on a pile of old newspapers stacked near the stove. Careless, that's what the fire crew would tell Frank in the morning, he surmised.

Swallowing the steaming cocoa, he reached for the timer in his pocket and the incendiary device hidden in his wallet. Quickly he wired them together and lit the fuse.

Then the drugs took effect.

The end

I have a number of writer friends, able to write wonderful romantic stories, a genre I seem unable to fulfil. However, here are a couple of my early efforts concerning love, but not the romantic sort.

About Suzanne

Tom gave a sigh of relief as he parked outside the college entrance. Suzanne, he never called her Sue, had phoned during the week to say she would be catching the six-thirty train home today, Friday. Deliberately, Tom had arranged to leave his office early in order to get to the college in good time to surprise her and give her a lift home in his new car. It had been a difficult journey, with road works, and slow moving vehicles on the motorway. but here he was at last, anticipating the warm hug she would give him and admonishing him with a laugh for his impatience to see her at the same time. As usual, she would be laden, it seemed to him, with a vast amount of essays and books, such a heavy load for his, so petite, girl. He could picture her now, rushing out of the building on her slender legs with her fair hair straying around her freckled face. It would be some thirty-five minutes before everyone left for the weekend, but he knew he would spot her immediately and, in any case she would have to pass the car to reach the nearby station. Tom opened the window a little and leaned back in his seat to wait.

Suzanne; his heart filled with love as he thought of her. He'd loved her, he told himself, from the moment he first saw her, but it was some months later when she had gazed at him with her clear blue eyes, smiled a dimpled smile and held out her arms that he knew he had fallen in love with her forever.

There was the time, he remembered when she had sobbed in his arms, for at least ten minutes because her dog had died, and then when he said they would go at the weekend and choose a puppy, she brightened at once. Despite this almost callous change, he recalled she quite often called the pup by the old dog's name.

They had their fair share of laughs too. Once, while crossing the stream, he slipped and fell into the water. How she laughed, and my how she shrieked when he came bearlike out of the water dripping wet and hugged her. Such wonderful memories to share.

At first, one by one people left the building, then there was a rush of them, some meeting up with the waiting friends, and Tom panicked that he might miss her. Within minutes the crowds had dispersed, and still she hadn't left the building. He began to worry, perhaps he had missed her after all. Then he saw her. So vulnerable looking, with her hair in two plaits, and some sort of mini dress over her trousers and a big bag of books dragging on her shoulder. She looked so

145

alive, radiant and happy. Tom thought, she's glad to be coming home.

He began to open the car door, when he saw someone step forward. Suzanne dropped her books and ran towards him, arms outstretched and he caught her, swept her off her feet and whirled her around. Then they kissed, a long lingering kiss.

Tom stepped back into the car, and as he sat down he felt a fleeting twist in his chest. Good grief, he thought, that's the first time I've ever felt jealous. Together they ambled towards the college gates, laughing at some joke together. As they got nearer to the car, Tom turned away. He was thankful that he was in the new car, and wouldn't be recognised. The lovers passed by, engrossed in each other giving no heed to the car that slowly drew away from the kerb into the stream of traffic.

Arriving home some two hours later, he was greeted at the door and handed a glass of beer by his wife, Marion, who said, 'Where on earth have you been? Dinner's been ready these last forty minutes.'

Tom took a welcome swallow of his beer, wiped his mouth, shrugged out of his jacket and collapsed onto a chair.

Excitedly she said, 'Well, did you get the new car? Does it run as smoothly as you've been saying it would?'

He pulled her down onto his knee. 'Yes, I've got the car and she's a beaut.' He kissed her and went on, 'Goes like a dream. Covered the miles endlessly.'

'What miles? Where have you been, Tom?'

He toyed with her fingers, sighed then shrugged his shoulders. 'I er ... I went to the college to meet Suzanne. Put the car through its paces and thought our grown-up daughter might like a lift home.'

The end

A Walk through the Woods

Carol, my mother suggested a walk. 'Through the woods, we haven't been there for a long time,' she said. It was our favourite walk and I readily agreed. We pulled on our wellies and tucked a bottle of water into our pockets. We took Bonnie, the dog, and as soon as we arrived she shot off chasing the squirrels. Carol and I sauntered our way along a well-trodden, muddy path that meandered between massive oaks, spindly hazels and grabbing brambles.

'Sit here a moment,' said Carol when we reached a fallen tree trunk. 'I have something to tell you.' Both of us reached for our water bottles and swallowed a mouthful. Carol took my hand and surprised, I looked at her.

She gave me a ghost of a smile and sighed. Softly, almost inaudibly she said, 'Your father and I are not your real parents.'

I gasped then half laughed. 'Oh, Mum,' I grinned at her. 'Every parent says that when their child has done something wrong, like as if they don't want to own them.'

She squeezed my hand.

'Come on, then. What have I done this time?'

She remained quiet for a few moments before saying, 'You were fifteen last week. We made up our minds that if things didn't alter while you were with us, we would tell you on your birthday.'

An unknown feeling almost of fear gripped me and I felt myself going cold as I asked, 'What do you mean?'

She was still clinging to my hand and said, 'You are Elizabeth's child, my sister. She came home to your gran's from London one day with you, only a few days old, in her arms. She told us nothing, nothing at all, and left the next day. She never came back for you so Frank and I registered you as ours.'

I pulled my hand out of hers absolutely dumbfounded. There was no mistaking what she had said. All of sudden, I wasn't me anymore. All sorts of thoughts raced through my mind. From this moment on I feared I had no father, mother, sisters or brother. All replaced in a moment with an uncle, aunt and cousins.

'We love you, Hannah, darling, you are and always will be our precious daughter. Please love, try to understand. We couldn't let you go to just anybody.'

For what like seemed an eternity neither of us spoke, then she said, 'Say something, Hannah. Nothing has or will change. You are our girl, our daughter.'

Now I was angry. I stood up quickly and walked back and forth before finally stopping in front of her. 'Why didn't you tell me from the start?' and before she could answer, I added, 'What a wicked thing to do abandon a baby – abandon me!'

'We, we …' began Carol.

'I heard the first time. Took pity on poor little, motherless me, didn't you? Not really yours am I?'

I heard her sigh, 'It wasn't like that at all. We …'

'I don't want to hear.' I snapped back. It was when I saw her stricken face that I sat down beside her. 'Sorry Mum,' I said softly, 'Didn't mean to hurt you. You're truly the best any girl could have.' We linked our fingers together and I put my head on her shoulder, 'Why didn't you tell me, though?'

'Because we were afraid of losing your love – your respect,' she replied. 'See how angry you were just now. We wondered, what would be the best for you and we decided to tell you on your fifteenth.'

For a few moments we sat quietly, each with our own thoughts, then I said, 'I want to see ... to see her, my birth mother.'

'Do you? Do you think that wise?'

'I need to see her, Mum. I need to understand why?' Carol nodded.

'Have you had any contact with her at all?'

'Well, I haven't seen her in a long while, but we do exchange Christmas cards so I have her address somewhere.'

I heard the bitterness in my voice as I asked, 'And I suppose she never asks after me?' Carol shook her head.

'And you never told her.'

'No, we thought as you grew, she might change her mind if she saw what a beautiful child you were. We loved you so much and just couldn't bear the idea of parting with you.'

'Tomorrow then, I will go and see her and give her a piece of my mind.'

'And I'll go with you.'

Elizabeth was only an hour's drive away it turned out. And when we reached Elizabeth's door the next day and before knocking, we hugged each other. 'It'll be alright, you'll see,' I whispered. When our knock was answered I was amazed to see a woman who, without doubt, had almost the same features as Carol, Grandma and me.

Elizabeth's face registered her shock at seeing us and her hand flew to her mouth. 'What are you doing here? What do you want?'

I didn't hesitate, 'I'm your daughter. Hannah.'

Elizabeth glanced quickly behind her and stared hard at Carol. 'Why, why have you done this?' she hissed at her. 'I have a family. They, no one knows of this ... this girl. I want no trouble.'

Carol smiled and reached out to her sister. 'Oh come on Lizzie, It's time I met this family of yours.'

I felt my heart leap with excitement. 'Does that mean I might have brothers and sisters?' I asked.

She glared at me before nodding.

'In that case, I should like to meet them.'

'Come on, Liz, invite us in. We won't stay long,' Carol pleaded.'

'No, I think not!' For a moment Elizabeth stood biting her lip and finally agreed. As she stepped aside to let us in she whispered, 'On one condition.'

I frowned and I asked, 'And what is that?'

'You do not, under any circumstances, tell who you are.'

It was Carol who nodded agreement.

'This way then,' and we followed her very stiff back until we reached the sitting room. She stopped for a moment and I saw the agonized look on her face, and as she opened the door I heard her hoarse whisper reminding us of the promise. We looked into the room and saw two girls around ten and twelve, giggling and wrestling a man to the floor, who was pleading for mercy.

Brightly Elizabeth called out, 'Hey, behave you two. Look who's come to see you. Your aunt Carol and … and …'

And before she could say anything more I said, 'Your big sister, Hannah.'

No one spoke. I saw the man, her husband frown then walk over to Elizabeth who had collapsed into a chair. I saw him bend over her and put his arm around her.

The elder of the two girls shyly asked, 'Really, truly? You are a secret sister?'

I nodded. Then the pair of them launched themselves at me. They hopped from foot to foot with excitement and were full of questions. I answered as truly and as carefully as I could. I didn't want to hurt Elizabeth any more who was now smiling up into her husband's face.

When it was time to leave, Carol said, 'Well, you can come and visit your sister whenever you like.'

'Yes,' I said, 'and we will take the dog for a long walk in the woods.'

I'm not sure if Elizabeth will ever truly accept me as her daughter but, in my mind, Carol and Frank are my true, loving parents.

The end

Another haiku, something I often inflicted on my babies.

Gentle soft brushing
Eyelashes on blushing cheek.
A flutter of love.

Meaningful and warm religious poetry is the chosen genre of another writer friend. I wrote the following when I was irritated by a Christian couple who, despite their commitment, cared for and helped only fellow worshippers at their church.

Of Some I Know

Do they deserve that inner peace
I see Sunday worshippers share.
I cannot commit myself,
I must be free
To express how much I care
For those in desperate need.
I give my time and expertise
As prayer alone I don't believe
Can all suffering be relieved.

These happy, well-fed, well-dressed
Healthy congregations,
Their love, their help, their support
For members only.
Not wed, divorced, live in sin.
No, we just don't want you in.
Oh yes! They contribute to
Relief in destroyed foreign lands,
Signing cheques – then wash their hands.

One alone showed the way,
Too many interpretations of His word.
No more will I listen to their say.
I know well the Prayer of the Lord,
The Ten Commandments, deadly sins,

Psalms and Creed.
These then shall my guidance be,
And trust my deeds will outweigh
My miserable faults on Judgement Day.

The end

One of the writers' societies I belong to set a competition, the results of which, will not be known until March, 2021. The subject was anything to do with the theatre profession. The word limit was two hundred and fifty words. I entered the following.

My Name in Lights

I dreamed of being a pop star. A career of singing and swaying hips, not to mention fabulous, outrageous costumes. But, overriding everything else, I dreamed of having my name in lights. I would have standing ovations, curtain calls and bouquets. There would be people pointing me out with awe as I waved from my limousine.

I dreamed of being presented to royalty, preferably the Queen, but Prince Philip might be more fun. Perhaps, I might be invited to Hollywood and without doubt, there would be generous contracts.

At first my family laughed when I held a large, silver serving spoon up to my mouth and mimed to any female singer on the television. It wasn't long before I mastered their dance routines and I truly began to feel my dream would become a reality. My voice was, it has to be said, a little out of tune, squeaky at times but I kept practising. Did I say, I am a little shy? I'd heard quite famous artists often are, so I was undaunted. Truth to tell, at my first audition I was struck dumb and fled the stage in tears. But the dream stayed with me down the years.

Today was the day. Here at last. The lifetime wait over. My name in lights. 'FRANCES TEMPLETON.' All around me there were fussy ripples, no actual applause but everyone stared as I stood up. I read the small print underneath – 'Dr. Johnson's room please'.

The end

My husband always chose to go to the coast for our holidays, whilst I preferred the countryside. We comprised, booked into a seaside resort, then had one day on the beach and the next ventured into the countryside. Our favourite venues were Devon or Suffolk. We did this routine throughout the two weeks away, weather permitting of course!

Country Senses

Owls tu-hooting,
Tractors trundling,
Farmhands whistling,
Wasps threatening,
Ripe corn rasping.
These are the sounds of the country.

Geese skeining,
Dogs rounding,
Snails silvering
Pigeons pilfering,
Dewdrops jewelling.
These are the sights of the country.

Onions pungenting,
Sillage spreading,
Foxes marking,
Cattle steaming,
Milk streaming.
These are the smells of the country.

Rump patting,
Lambs' wool curling,
Trout tickling,
Goats butting,
Nettles stinging.
These can be felt in the country

Cream strawberrying,
Bilberries staining,
Elderflower champagning,
Apples sweetening,
Beans running,
These are the tastes of the country.

The end

A number of readers will be familiar with the National Service, when after the Second World War conscription was compulsory for men at eighteen years old. Del was a good friend, a cockney barrow-boy, with a dubious reputation, but always very loyal to his many friends. He was full of stories of his past and here is one of his true tales.

Del's Story

This is a true account of my friend Derek Fisher, not his real name as I fear he might get into trouble should the authorities ever choose to investigate. Derek was brought up by his sister, Pamela who was fifteen years his senior. Needless to say Derek was not only spoilt but smothered in love. So much so, that at nearly eighteen he was longing for his National Service call-up papers to get away from home and have an adventure.

At last in 1954 after the compulsory medical, the long awaited papers finally arrived in a brown envelope with 'Her Majesty's Service' stamped on the outside. Excitedly Derek had opened it and gasped. His sister took the papers from him and shocked, said, 'Bloody hell.'

They agreed there must be some mistake. Derek told me later that Pamela asked everyone what was going to happen to her lad? Had the army gone mad and, more hopefully, they don't mean it do they?

Derek's call-up papers had said he was to join the Irish Fusiliers in Omagh, Northern Ireland. The papers also explained that he had to report to Liverpool to board the boat the following week. There was constant news at the time of the Irish Republican Army reforming and determined to make trouble.

Derek got in touch with the authorities to see if they'd got it right. At that time, he didn't have a telephone, nor did any of the neighbours, so he went to the public phone at the bottom of the road, armed with a pocketful of pennies and sixpences to speak to the recruiting officer. When he returned to Pamela after the fruitless call he had to tell her reluctantly that the officer had insisted there was no mistake. As he told me he mimicked the loud, fierce voice he'd heard and repeated, 'Get yourself to Liverpool lad as ordered, or find yourself in big trouble. Understand?'

To be honest, Derek told me later after there was no hope of the destination, Amarh Barracks, being changed that he hadn't cared where he was going, as long as it was out of Ruislip.

Pamela had sighed as she reminded him that at least he knew one end of a rifle from the other and that he'd have no bother looking after himself. 'Just make sure you aim as well as before.'

Here Derek laughed as he told me, 'I knew what she was referring to.' Seems a friend had lent him an air rifle and he had gone upstairs and fired it, more than once, out of the window. It was in the evening that the police called to say that someone had complained about an air rifle being fired during the day. He confessed and was duly cautioned at the station the next morning. Again he laughed. 'The street was very quiet at the time until Mrs Gardener, a rather plump woman, made her way past the house. So, I thought, I'd have a pot shot when she was further down the road, and guess what? I hit her full on the bum.' He went on to say that he had ducked down when she turned round, all red in the face, very angry, but he was sure he hadn't been spotted.

Derek went on to tell me of his short time over in Ireland. Being around five foot four and a half inches, not an average height, when he arrived in Liverpool, he told me, 'Every b...r was over six foot! Put the fear of God in me,' and there and then he expected to be sent home. 'To be fair,' he told me, 'the lads were sympathetic, took me under their wing and made me their mascot.' When he arrived at the garrison with the new recruits, the officer in charge admitted there must have been a mistake and he would arrange for a transfer but couldn't say when. For the time being, he was confined to barracks along with everyone else. The British army was loathed and every soldier a target.

For a moment, Derek was quiet, then chuckled before going on. 'One Saturday afternoon, I was playing cards with the boys. We were lounging around on my bed which was between a small cupboard on one side to keep my things in, and a tall, steel locker on the other side for my clothes. They were bloody noisy when you were a kip and someone banged into one in the dark. So, there we were laughing and cheating when someone rushed in and yelled out, "Guess what, the I.R.A. are raiding our armoury."'

Derek handed me a well worn piece of newspaper and I read, 'There was a raid on Omagh Barracks, Tyrone, in which an I.R.A. party attempted to reprise the highly valued British war material from Gough Barracks, Armagh, in June'.

Derek continued with his tale. 'All those blokes picked up their weapons and rushed out,' he said grinning. 'Everyone I knew who had completed their conscription stint told me that whatever I did, never volunteer for anything as one could easily be tricked into all sorts of, usually unpleasant, tasks. So when I heard what this bloke said, I leapt, honestly leapt into the locker and said, "B...r that".'

I laughed, and asked him what happened afterwards.

'Well, after a bit I heard the others shouting for me, "Where's Kip?" I thought to myself, if they think I'm going out there to sort out the Irish they can think again.

'I'm in here,' I yelled back, 'and I'm staying here until they've gone. I could hear them all laughing and then one said, "Come out you daft s.d, they've gone."'

I asked him why they call him Kip and he told me that because he was not having enough to eat and not getting out much, all he could do was sleep or kip as the lads used to say. 'If they wanted me, they'd look on my bed first.'

It wasn't long after that Derek got his transfer to Aldershot. It seems the food in the Armagh Barracks was so awful that he couldn't eat it and when he arrived at his new barracks he was put on double rations as he was so undernourished.

Pamela was in tears when she heard this. 'They should have sent you home to me,' she said. 'I'd have seen you were properly fed. None of that army muck.' Derek said he'd laughed as he told her that whatever he fancied in the mess he was given double helpings twice and soon put on weight.

Pamela wasn't satisfied. One day, Derek said, whilst kipping on his bed at Aldershot, a voice boomed down the hut, 'Fisher you're wanted in the guardhouse. At the double.'

Not sure what he had done to invite a visit to the guard room, it was 'At the Double' he made his way there.

When he entered, one of the military police hiding a grin pointed and said, 'It's your mother.'

Derek was shocked to see his sister who had told him that she was worried he wasn't getting enough to eat so had bought some smoked salmon and some chicken sandwiches. Derek said just for a moment he forgave her for embarrassing him in front of the police and the one chap in the guardhouse. Although he dearly would like to have wiped the grin off the face of the guard he told him it was his sister, not his muvver.

Looking forward to the treats his sister had brought, he put his hand out for the sandwiches which he knew would have been packed neatly and with care as was Pamela's way, but there were none. It seems the prisoner had spun her a yarn about being starved as part of his punishment and she, feeling sorry for him, parted with Derek's feast.

Derek served the rest of his time in Egypt. Between being a batman for an Irish major, he entertained the troops as a member of Entertainment National Service Association.

The end

Just to make you smile!

A Limerick

Her hair was not bleached but toned,
Her breasts not pads, silliconed.
The face though not gifted
Was better uplifted,
La Belle, 'til his beard was full grown.

The end

Yesss!

I was sorry to hear
You'd lost your husband, dear.
I smiled weakly, gave thanks with a nod
Lost. Not him, the selfish old sod.
He's not very far,
Over there, in the black jar.

What was lost was my life
When he made me his wife,
Come here, go there,
Fetch this and fetch that.
Each child was a brat.

But soon for me a new life begins.
I'll scatter his ashes without violins.
But no, that's too good for one who has sinned.
So I'll tip his remains in a smelly trash bin.

The end

I do hope you found all within this book, interesting, informative and occasionally amusing.

Finding, and reading again, forgotten work, some dating back to 2006, and collating the material with my chat links, has been surprisingly rewarding. I might even have enough material for another book.

My more recent work has mainly been for children, including the life of a child on canal boats in the early twentieth century (three books). These were written because I was appointed children's storyteller for Hillingdon Narrowboats Society. Needless to say, much research was needed. These were followed by the adventures of a Welsh boy during the difficult times of the nineteen seventies (six books).

So that you close this book with a smile, here are some anecdotes that my friend has agreed I may share with you.

Frances Funnies

Frances is a keen walker and enjoys investigating anything unusual. One day she went to the local House and Gardens and as she strolled around, she spotted a fallen tree trunk with an unusual 'fungus'. The trunk was at the top of a sloping bank. As it had been raining, the ground was wet and muddy, and not once but a number of times, she slipped. At last, she reached the trunk, only to find that the 'fungus' was a wet, shrivelled up leather glove.

Frances in her late 70s, was taken out for the evening by her family. First, they visited a local country inn. Frances settled herself in a comfortable chair for the evening, but the family had other ideas. They, including Frances, went on to, as she puts it, a 'rave'. Laughing, she said, 'I was on my feet from about 8.30 p.m. to eleven.' The family were amazed at her stamina, as she danced alongside them, and asked how she liked the music. She answered, 'Music? I just followed what you were doing. I didn't hear the music, I had my earplugs in.'

Another time Frances took her sons to a Christmas Parade. The floats went by, depicting various pantomimes and customs, the last being, she thought, Dracula, in a hooded long gown. 'Look,' she said to her boys, 'Dracula.' Imagine how embarrassed she was when Dracula turned to her and said, 'Madam, I am the local vicar.'

I was walking with Frances to the local shops, one very hot summer's day and we passed a couple of workmen digging a hole. We were not long in the shop and on our way home within five minutes. When we reached the working men, she said, 'You still here?' One wiped his brow, swallowed water from a bottle and then replied with a laugh, 'There's a pick in the van, Missus, if you've a mind to get the job done quicker.' If I hadn't dragged her away, I reckon she would have had a go!

Most Christmases Frances stays with her son and his growing family. This means a train journey, including some changes. One Christmas her young grandson bought her a potted plant. Time to go home, thought Frances and her grandson escorted her to the station proudly carrying the plant. He handed it over at the barrier and Frances thought, What to do? How am I going to carry this and my full and heavy carrier bag? Dearly she would have liked to dump it, but knew better! What to do? Then she had an inspiring moment, she stuffed her laundry, panties mainly, into her pockets and made room for the potted plant. Very resourceful and the plant is still blooming.

2019, Frances has a mobile phone, and can manage calls and texts, but is not altogether familiar with the digital world and is often surprised at what is being achieved. Walking round a well-known shop she came across underwire bras. She said she was astounded to think that women could access a wireless through their underwear. The truth dawned on her when she came to the section displaying wire-less bras!

Frances had a puzzle. Why couldn't she get the front door open? It took her a few moments to realise she had the key to the back door in her hand.

Lunching with Frances and our friend Jenny, our talk turned to the new season's jersey potatoes. Frances told us the following. She was with David, her husband, having dinner in a restaurant and the menu stated fresh vegetables. David was convinced the potatoes were not new and an argument ensued with the waitress. The exchange ended when she emphatically said, 'Yes, they are new it says so on the tin!' Another lunchtime. Frances told us she once went to a Hen Party and that a group of handsome men appeared. She thought they were called after a tree, 'Something like chestnuts,' she said. Her choice of a tree caused us all to laugh and Jenny explained she meant, The Chippendales!

The end

And finally, a word of warning readers, if you see someone with a pen and paper scribbling furiously, it might be me or a fellow author, so be very careful when chatting with others, especially in public places.

Books by Beatrice

Children
The Adventures of Rhys:
  Training a Greyhound
  Urgent! Pocket Money Required
  Disasters and Delights of Family Celebrations
  The Sometimes Society
  Enormous Responsibilities
  When Rhys Fell out a Tree

Towpath Tale series
  Towing Path Tales
  More Towing Path Tales
  A Particular Year

Adult
A Man from the North East
Elusive Destiny
Archie's Children

Plays by Beatrice

A Certain Monday
Connie's Lovely Boy
From Commoner to Coronet
Governed by Magpies
In Less than Ten Minutes
Plays for Young Actors

www.ingramcontent.com/pod-product-compliance
Lightning Source LLC
Chambersburg PA
CBHW051344020726
47501CB00007B/2265